HONEYEATER

ALSO BY

Kathleen Jennings

Flyaway

Kindling: Stories

Travelogues: Vignettes from Trains in Motion

Honeyeater

Kathleen Jennings

TOR

TOR PUBLISHING GROUP
NEW YORK

HONEYEATER

Interior illustrations by Kathleen Jennings

A Tor Book
Published by Tom Doherty Associates / Tor Publishing Group
120 Broadway
New York, NY 10271

www.torpublishinggroup.com

Tor® is a registered trademark of Macmillan Publishing Group, LLC.

EU Representative: Macmillan Publishers Ireland Ltd, 1st Floor, The Liffey Trust Centre, 117–126 Sheriff Street Upper, Dublin 1, DO1 YC43

The Library of Congress Cataloging-in-Publication Data is available upon request.

ISBN 978-1-250-84588-7 (hardcover)
ISBN 978-1-250-84589-4 (ebook)

Our books may be purchased in bulk for specialty retail/wholesale, literacy, corporate/premium, educational, and subscription box use. Please contact MacmillanSpecialMarkets@macmillan.com.

First Edition: 2025

Printed in the United States of America

10 9 8 7 6 5 4 3 2 1

For Angela and Rebecca

HONEYEATER

CHAPTER ONE

Flood Nights

Flood nights are dark, but not silent.

The water itself is quiet, rising like black glass, although at sunset it was the tobacco-amber of old bottles. The creek feels its way between crepe myrtles and kurrajongs and ripples by finger-widths up Volney Street, pushing blood-warm air ahead of it. There is not yet any stench of mud. For a few hours, the newly submerged trees, the grass and gardens smell of life.

The suburb of Bellworth sits in a pocket of land laced around by a creek of the same name, and scored by its tributaries—ditches and weed-choked creases behind backyards. The creek, when low, is a reedy meander, skein-ing towards the deep churn of Gowburgh River, many sub-urbs away.

Now it is swollen into one body. On the other side cattle bellow, startling in a city. Beyond that unlikely marsh of paddocks, warehouses sink, and a single alarm rings unan-swered and unsilenceable. Above, helicopters grind towards somewhere else. Closer, there is a splash—clammy coils or draggled pelt making for higher ground.

This is one of the nights the creek makes its own. The houses that always flood (every hundred, every thirty-five, every seven years) are thick with a soup of clothes and books and chipboard, tainted with what the water carries. At times wavelets glimmer: starlight, perhaps, or someone's torch.

And islanded at the top of Volney Street, on chairs and crates in the middle of the road, sit those of us who remain. (Only one neighbour—a taxi driver who never talks to us—stays in his house with a battery lantern.)

Their first names blur and trade from one generation to the next—no need to remember those. But the surnames you will recognise from signs and parks and shops across Bellworth. Here are the current Braithes, who built their house when they were young, when Mr Braithe would ride home along a dirt track, beams balanced across his bicycle. There is Mr Eising, widower, and Joe and Joanne (his son and daughter-in-law), who live downhill in a house bought from a cousin; Edith Tepping, whose house meets the lane that runs past the school and graveyard, and who is so old even the Braithes defer to her. And there is, of course, a Wren, sprawled quiet on a folding chair, long hands interlaced behind light brown hair.

We look at the lowered stars, and dredge up stories we once knew, or borrowed, or stole: the hauntings of Bellworth, reconstituted by water.

Out in the depths, where the current drags silt and grief inexorably away, something thrashes and is gone.

And everyone has a tale.

The First Day

GRAVEYARD TAG

Of course, it didn't help that the school's built between a cemetery and a war memorial (says an Eising, perhaps Joanne). Games turned ghoulish.

There was Sally-in-the-well. Whoever was "Sally" had to answer three questions truthfully. Then they'd break the circle of linked arms and chase the interrogator all the way home. There was the one where the Doctor replaced one patient's soul with a bird, and another's with a cat (by whispering in their ears), and you'd have to work out who was who.

What about graveyard tag? (says her husband). If you were caught, you fell down and grabbed the ankles of kids running by. The last survivor would be the next game's murderer. They banned that after a student broke their teeth on a gravestone.

And blood-in-water (says Joanne), to summon the spirit of the Butcher of Bellworth.

The principal called a special assembly to stop us talking about ghosts. But what could he do? Once someone claimed they'd heard their name rasped at midnight beneath their bedroom window, everyone started hearing whispers.

CHAPTER TWO

Home

Gowburgh, of which Bellworth is one fragment, was—is—a river city, its light thick with humidity and rich as coloured glass. Foliage and flowers (spun-sugar, silk-velvet), blue-mirrored offices and tin-roofed houses foam the shores of its river. They rise along myriad gullies and flash like sun on waves.

For most of his life, Charlie Wren—who, tall and brown-haired, should have been distressingly unremarkable in Gowburgh—had intended to leave. But although he had spent years escaping to friends, to part-time jobs, over bridges, through tunnels, he had never succeeded in moving away. He'd blinked and a year, a decade slid by.

Today, he looped across the suburbs by bus and train, crawlingly aware of the approach of Bellworth Creek. Charlie, always conscious of waterways (life-threading, death-steeped), could have followed them with his eyes closed.

And it was good to be out of his share house. For the last month, since the police had (again) asked him *not to leave Gowburgh at this time*, he'd been pretending. For the sake of curious housemates he'd performed moderate concern about his acquaintance (if that was the right word) Alli's abrupt disappearance; he'd told himself things would be okay; he'd acquired for the last two weeks a veneer of decent sombreness after his aunt Ida died. It was a relief to stop acting.

And quietly, he *was* worried about Alli, not just because the police were. But, as his older sister reminded him, and as he had dutifully convinced himself and the police, he and Alli hadn't known each other well (despite his sister's encouragement at the time) or for long—and people often left. His aunt, however, had raised Charlie and Cora. And while Wrens, as his sister reassured him, did not feel things deeply, housemates and detectives did not understand that.

But the inheritance from Ida meant he was nearly free of all that. After he'd announced he was moving out, his room had been re-let with unflattering haste and he'd spent the last night on a too-short sofa (housemates, like detectives, became cold when people you knew had a tendency to go missing). His possessions were in a bag on the seat beside him, and as far as he knew, emptying their aunt's house was Cora's only current scheme involving him. He was between jobs he'd never intended to keep and was broke, true. But once they sold the property, once the police lost interest again and Alli sent a message to someone, he'd be gone—away from this city, and its creeks that haunted his dreams with deaths not his own. Charlie promised himself this was the last time he'd go home.

He had suggested they sell the house—cluttered long before Aunt Ida's last slow illness—as-was. Cora, smiling, had said, "You never know what people might find." Charlie knew better than to keep secrets. They'd be dug up by someone who hoped Charlie was as interesting as his sister, or who—based on his recurrent appearance in their investigations as known associate or last-person-to-see or (once) prior victim or person-who-found-the-corpse—suspected that he'd done something *too* interesting. But Cora, rising in council politics, couldn't afford even other people's secrets.

The hills of latticed houses with sunset burned into their shadows fell away. The other passenger in the carriage—a man burdened with key chains—dozed and did not judge him. The train swayed into a cream brick station built when Bellworth was farms, ejected Charlie, and lurched away.

Gowburgh, which had absorbed Bellworth a century before, had not dissolved it. Although from some rooftops you could glimpse a shard of the city centre, hazed silver, it would seem another world. Charlie, bag over his shoulder, strode into Station Road, angling down towards Bellworth Road and the creek. Although the decline was gentle, when water rose a metre's difference became stark.

First were the shops, the tidy library, and a sensation of being watched. And then, like a map, the streets unfolded around him.

It was a golden day. Seedpods clattered, lost-bird posters fluttered on power poles. Above corrugated iron rooftops, flame trees burned away to jacaranda smoke (*in the branches,* said a long-ago voice, *are Chattering Jacks, their eyes too green in the night . . .*). But the branches were busy with birds—blue-faced honeyeaters flicking flowers up to get at the nectar, noisy miners falling and reeling grey-and-yellow on the breeze.

Charlie was reluctantly buoyed. Alli had bullied him towards happiness, but today for a moment there was a swing in his step he'd last felt at fourteen, before nightmares of drownings (his, and others') began to wake him.

Then the ground dipped and a phantom torrent pressed on his lungs, and the rest of boyhood rushed back, stale with disappointments.

In power lines over the ibis-haunted floodplains, the wind sang. (*And there I saw, shimmering in the middle of the reeds* . . . it was Liddy-down-the-hill's voice.) Between high-set houses, a culvert cut under footpath and road. A spill of moss hinted at standing water (*and clever words, whispering out of the tunnel* . . . said that long-ago Liddy, her square freckled face gleeful).

There was a shortcut over a footbridge. He hadn't had a reason to take that path since Liddy and her family moved out of Bellworth. And since those days he'd learned to be prepared to explain his movements. First, about the old man at the Drowned House, whose death he shouldn't regret, and then others, who'd been friends before vanishing: Stef McNally, good company and a terrible barista. Jess Poll, easy in all things, except returning. Micah Chave, whose friendship had got him through university, and whom he'd discovered in the river—the only return Charlie couldn't hope for. Others, perhaps, who had been the cause of more oblique enquiries. Unless he recited their names, their faces blended into a composite *Missing* poster. And now, Alli, gone in . . . what? A bad mood, a spirit of adventure, a struggle in the water?

Liddy's was the only departure for which he hadn't needed an alibi.

So Charlie kept to the footpath, past high fences he could look over easily now, their wire and timber and tin garlanded with passionfruit, while sunlight gleamed on mango leaves or was diffused through bottlebrush.

His aunt's house was at the far end of the suburb. Braithe and Eising Streets looped off the main road, around the primary school and down to the creek. Where they met, Volney rose, ending at the tiny heritage cemetery, and the lane that cut behind the ovals.

Somewhere, he heard kids playing a game. How did it go? Caliban? Calabash?

> *Whoever-it-was, empty as a gourd,*
> *Teeth as sharp as a hatchet,*
> *What would you eat for lunch*
> *If only you could catch it?*

And while the others crept nearer, *It* (eyes closed) declared *honeycomb-and-gravy* or *curried-sausages-and-ice-cream* or *wedding-cake-and-green-beans*, until at last they shouted *YOU*, and the chase was on.

Alli would have snorted at him—*if you'd focus on the present, you might make something of yourself.* He'd have almost believed it.

In the cemetery, the eroding surnames were the same as on the suburb's war memorial, parks, and signs: Braithe, Eising, Damson, Tepping. But mostly Wrens, closer as a family in death than living. Charlie tapped each headstone as he passed (died young, died old, died quick, died cold, moved slow, was bold). *Child*, he thought in his sister's voice, although she'd taught him the rhyme. At least Aunt Ida's ashes weren't here. Charlie wiped his hand on his shirt and stepped into Volney Street.

A dead-end street, quiet, avoided equally by traffic and the worst winds and hail, it arced down the shoulder of the world, plunging to the overgrown reserve that hid the creek. Charlie felt the water lurking, an olive-green slick flecked with sky like fallen leaves.

Up here he could breathe. The survivors of what had once been an avenue of magpie-haunted jacarandas canopied the houses. And at the crest, ever above flood level, was the gate to number 21.

SEEDPODS

When I was little, says Edith dreamily, my cousin cracked seed-pods that fell too soon. Leopard-tree pods polished and hard; frog-mouthed jacaranda purses; boat-shaped bottle-tree cases, harlequin beetles clinging like shields along the sides. Gumnuts fallen with their caps still on.

He'd stamp on them, burst them open. You don't know what might hatch, he'd say.

But one year, after the big storm, there were so many seed-pods, fallen green. Too many.

My parents wouldn't talk about my cousin, after that. And I never saw him again.

CHAPTER THREE

The Creek

In the darkness before a dawn, Bellworth Creek—strangled, invaded by netted roots—finally choked on itself.

It retched mud, which sprouted teeth, clawed free of weeds, vomited out its own water, and became not-creek. Wet leaves tightened around a restless musculature of vines.

It opened its eyes.

The green sky pearlesced into day. The thing knew that word. And knowing *day*, it knew it was alive.

For a time, that immense in-gasping knowledge was enough. The thing-that-was-not-dead lay cradled in reeds, while air bellowed its cracking ribs, and the lives in the trees passed through its mirroring gaze.

Having no feathers—not the honeyeater's olive blue, nor a galah's rose pink, nor the pallor of a great heron—it understood it was not a bird. It was not a diving rakali, for it had hair instead of fur. Dogs barked, and it did not answer, for it was not a dog.

It wondered at the small planes that tossed overhead, and jagged edges of memories grated together in its drying skull. Under a high sun, as mud flaked from its skin, it watched a person in burred skirts tramp the opposite bank, a dog (perhaps) at her heels. One afternoon, shrieks rang in the trees—it recalled *help,* and then *children.*

Crouched between a rotten log and a stand of bamboo, it howled an answer rank and strange. The children, who like their parents had populated the creek with monsters, stampeded away.

⟋⟍

Evening. Windows gleamed uphill, where lay something the creature had held almost as tightly as life.

The dusk was thick with insects, the grass rippled with toads. Desperation rose from the creek, scrabbling for space inside the skin of this *thing-that-was-alive.*

But the thing—the person—was learning the edges of itself. Words budded in its mouth. *Mine,* it thought fiercely. It found the children's shelter, and in it a rag it recognised as a dress—a barrier against the hungry night.

⟋⟍

Day, and the person staggered up to the joining of three streets. They saw houses, the restless fog of humidity glazing the road, the net of Bellworth taut over older patterns. And they remembered, bitter as unused breath, another word:

Wren.

CHATTERING JACKS

There was once a boy who was rude, and bad, and ungovernable (says someone, every flood night, but Charlie heard it first from Ida). One evening, marauding home through Tepping Park, he stumbled into a conference of Chattering Jacks.

Chattering Jacks have round curious faces and brush-soft tails like possums, though their hands are cleverer. They chitter snidely in the bushes, and you must never talk back.

But the boy did not freeze. He jeered and sneered at each remark, and finally the beasts would take no more. They ruffled their hackles, their eyes gleamed green, and their cat-claws glinted. The boy clicked his teeth shut, and did the worst thing: he ran.

They shouted behind him the whole way home. Under the stairs and at the windows, they mocked. Beneath his floor and in the ceiling, they scritch-scritch-scratched. Until dawn, they taunted:

"Run if you will, hide if you can,
You will never know silence again."

For the rest of his life, he couldn't bear to be alone. If he was, wherever he was, he'd hear claws scrape, and voices whispering:

"Run if you will, hide if you can,
You will never know silence again."

CHAPTER FOUR

Number 21

The house was screened by mock-orange and jasmine, their scents heavy as a drug. Vines wove the front gate's rusting scrollwork, and sprung under the weight of birds.

Charlie gently untwisted tendrils from the latch, then shoved the gate through overlong grass.

The house, velvety with flaking paint, slumped on timber posts as tall (in front) as Charlie. Scalloped palings and ferns filled the space between them. Behind those, beneath the squared, plank floor of the high building, hulked shadows. The downpipes were cut—roots must have blocked the drains. From the patchwork roof, magpies watched calmly. His sister had said the structure was sound; they'd advertise it as a renovator's dream.

Low on the verandah steps were a bag of grapefruit, a box of eggs, and a mustard jar with . . . Charlie picked it up. An avocado pit, suspended by toothpicks across the mouth, was already letting down a thready root. Gifts from the neighbours.

Charlie climbed to the latticed verandah door, and before he unlocked it, lifted a hand towards the street. But he hoped no one saw. He didn't plan on staying to be befriended.

Spiderwebs fogged the outer balustrades. On the inner wall of the verandah were casement windows; their pressed glass, backed by darkness, had the sheen of boiled jam— amber, mulberry, bottle green.

The rooms behind were a verandah once, too. And that was not the first to have been enclosed. 21 Volney Street had grown like the rings of a tree.

Charlie crossed to the true front door and let himself in.

⚜

He took the central hallway through the labyrinth. Cora had messaged, breezily, for him to throw out Ida's things, just save any family papers for her to check. She'd added, "You won't know what's important."

In the orange kitchen at the back, last redecorated in Ida's youth, he displaced a cup of paintbrushes and forced the window open. Once the rusty water ran clear, he re-filled the avocado-seed jar and placed it on the sill, then looked around.

A yellowed advertisement for Bellworth Estate Subdivisions, a bare century old, still hung proudly above a chrome-sided table piled with strips of newspaper. Ill-matched knives angled drunkenly into the knife block. One high cupboard was full of bottles, which Charlie poured out before he could change his mind.

The food in the fridge, however, was fresh. Cora, be-tween meetings, had had time to doubt Charlie's ability to feed himself. He was nettled. But Cora would have said in-dependence wasn't always a virtue, and *had* he remembered to buy food?

He opened the back door. The rear of the house was

higher, and long stairs descended to the yard: shed, clothes-line, and dense trees. Jacaranda flowers fell where his mother used to sit in the short time after she'd discovered that, in spite of Ida's cold care, she was dying. He faintly pictured petals reflected, dissolving, in the dark blue ring that hung loose on her thin hand. (Or had that been on Ida's mottled hand, on his mother's shoulder? And where was that ring, now?)

After that, until he'd almost been drowned, Charlie spent his childhood hiding in those branches (Ida's dog, Dennis, sleeping below), or at Liddy's, or by the creek.

The house was pulling him under. *Keep moving,* he told himself (Liddy's voice, leading him astray). *Make a list of what needs to be done* (Alli's, trying to reform him, almost succeeding). *Breathe.*

He went back in, and surveyed the rooms.

The space Aunt Ida once grudged her niece and nephew had been reabsorbed, and the air was musty with old illness, sourer than even a filthy share house, more human than Cora's sterile apartment.

"She'd have liked to be rid of us," Cora had said. "But it's our time, now."

First, the cemetery side. Nearest the front door was the study, mountainous with papers, then the sewing room stuffed with splitting bags of cloth. Through narrow doors set with mottled glass was the enclosed verandah that had been Charlie's.

Next on that side were Cora's old bedroom, locked, and Ida's. Charlie entered meaning to look for Ida's sapphire ring, the one thing he'd had half an idea Alli might like. The room, however, brimmed with clothes and a scent mingled of camphor and old dog. It was so thick he felt as if hands (rippling in shadowy mirrors) pushed him out into the hallway.

He could not remember which room had been his mother's. His image of her in the house was hazy; he recalled a voice, but no words.

The narrow toilet was cantilevered off the side of the house, its cistern mounted near the ceiling. Next—and last, before the kitchen—was the bathroom, the enamel of its claw-footed tub bruised. The shower curtain was a dank, translucent membrane mottled with mould. It clung to Charlie's arms as he bundled it beside the mint-coloured sink.

It was a start.

But the creekward side of the house was a spiral of fossilised verandahs, forgotten bedrooms, and drawers of projects. Peeling wardrobes stooped under high ceilings, while conduits and wiring skinned with paint corded the grooved timber walls. Breezeways cast fretwork shadows, and draughts puffed stale through the boards from the vast space below the floor (big as a house, again).

The linen cupboard, its door cut out of the vertical planks and latched with wire, opened onto floral sheets old before Charlie was born, and fraying towels, and the faint cool scent of detergent and memory. But everything else in the house smelled of glue and arrested decay. Charlie, awaiting an official knock at the door, drifted among skeletal wire maquettes, tiny models of the station and library, boxes of weathered bones. The police would be at best sarcastic about those. He wondered, too, if he should wear cleaning gloves, and decided that would look worse.

It's just art, he practised saying.

⚜

Ida, rarely one for stories, had told Charlie and Cora about an artist famed for painting animals with such scientific precision that people who attended his exhibitions were afraid they'd be attacked.

What people didn't see (said Ida) was the laboratory where he dissected his subjects, the better to understand them. They didn't know about scalpels dark with dried blood, tufts of fur caught in the cracks of the workbench.

One day, a parliamentarian who was (by various means) becoming important, decided to have his picture painted by this artist. After much flattery and money, and although (or because) the artist did not like the man's politics, he agreed.

The final artwork caught the petty genius, the corrupting appetites of its subject, and became famous for two reasons. First because it won, with the usual controversy, an important prize. Second because, shortly before it was completed, the politician vanished. *Corruption and villainy,* people whispered, not quite shocked. *Blackmail and spies.*

The portrait hangs at Parliament House. No body was ever found.

Cora, then at an age to be charmed by the ghoulish, was delighted. Charlie had regarded art—and artists—with suspicion ever since. He suspected that when the police next surprised him with a visit, they would do the same.

⚜

Finally, he reached the parlour, the oldest room. It was windowless, and had a fireplace at one end, which he'd never seen lit, and a chimney through which birds had fallen until

Ida had it blocked up. Underneath the floorboards a sturdy brick pillar supported it, but when Charlie was small, Cora had told him the chimney went down, down, *all* the way down.

He switched on the fringed lamp, and shadows spidered the walls. Badly tinted photographs of past Wrens glared. Charlie couldn't name them. The velour sofas were badly sprung. The single bookshelf held encyclopaedias, spines glinting like coins in mud, and a handful of unfortunate souvenirs. And for a moment, he thought a dog pressed against his leg.

But Dennis had sickened and died years ago. There was nothing there.

The Second Day

THE COCKATOO

Jim, the old mechanic (says Mrs Braithe), kept a cockatoo in a cage that took up half his back verandah. I don't know why; there are plenty wild in Gowburgh. Although, to be fair, you see hardly any around here—only flying over high and fast, screaming like rusty gates.

He taught it to talk, and when he was at work, you'd hear it chatting to itself. "Who's a pretty creature? You're a pretty creature. Am I? Yes, you are, you are, you are."

Well, in time it died, as natural a death as something can that's lived its whole life in a cage. Jim got over it soon enough.

But for a while, on days when I was gardening along the fence that joined Jim's yard, I'd hear a voice saying, "Who's a pretty creature? Am I? Am I? Am I?" Waiting for an answer that never came.

CHAPTER FIVE

Paper

Charlie, feet hanging off his old bed, rested badly. Experience made him wait for a late-night knock on the door, an inquisition that never came. He did hear, however, quite clearly, Ida walk down the hallway.

It was the house shifting. Rooms away, the refrigerator gasped and settled into a torturous rattle. Once the wardrobe door slipped off its latch and eased open. Below the bare floor, something shuffled and clinked: noises he had, as a boy, attributed to the dog. Charlie missed having a living thing to blame. Would it occur to Alli, returning unaware of the panic, to tell him everything was fine?

"Just possums," he told the sloping ceiling.

When he did sleep, the scale of the task crashed over him. Accumulated leavings of Wrens avalanched unceasingly, dust forcing its way under his eyelids, into his nostrils, through his clenched teeth. Then a familiar too-green, silt-silken sleep, in which his own hands held drowners under the mud, which he enjoyed even less.

Charlie woke sweating in coloured sunlight, with a headache from heat and nightmares.

Something stank.

In the hallway, a reek of death gusted past. He followed it to the kitchen. It was fainter, but he suspected the drain.

Charlie wolfed a piece of bread, plain, to settle his stomach, then looked under the sink. The plumbing was iridescent with corrosion. He rapped a pipe experimentally and a toll, like a bell beneath the house, answered. He struck another with a spoon. A tone higher.

He'd lived with enough engineering students and apprentice tradies to know this path led to expensive mistakes. Yet for once, there was no landlord to answer to. Charlie, folded into the cupboard, brightened. Let Cora scold him—only half the house was hers.

A touch feathered across his face.

Spiders. Charlie dealt his head a ringing blow on the underside of the sink, tangled his legs among the kitchen chairs and for a moment, trapped, could not inhale. He kicked free. The table slammed against a cabinet, rattling Aunt Ida's dinner sets.

Charlie, flat on the floor, willed his heart to slow. Something ticked and scrabbled in the roof—bird claws on iron, or a scaly uncoiling in the insulation. He stood up, counting breaths, and put the kettle on.

Then he retraced the stink to where it was strongest. In the high hallway ceiling was a hatch.

As he fetched a ladder, Charlie reflected that he should have travelled interstate with everyone—anyone—the police asked him about. With Alli, who'd flipped a silver charm to decide whether to leave this year. With Jess, who'd left before Charlie was introduced to Alli over too-sweet cocktails. That would have solved his problems. Or if he'd cleared out with Stef-at-the-café, who'd gone hitchhiking and probably had a perfectly pleasant adventure. Or, all the way back, he should have run off with Liddy as they'd planned, before she abandoned him.

At least he'd never dreamed Liddy's death. Nor, when he went into the water, did he imagine her, drowned, brushing against him. Of all of them, it was easiest to believe Liddy (irrepressible, haloed in memory by copper-bright hair) survived.

Time was sliding again. Just this one favour for Cora, he reassured himself. Even if she hadn't reminded him of her sacrifices, she'd have been entitled to ask for something much less reasonable. After that, he'd really leave.

When he was small, he'd climbed trees higher than the house. He'd scaled the narrower hallway in Liddy's house with hands and feet braced against opposite walls. The ladder, now, felt more precarious. Steadying himself, Charlie stretched up. He fitted his fingers against previous fingerprints on the cover and lifted. The hatch opened with an unmistakable scent not of death but of dried plants—brittle leaf-shards and shrivelled jacaranda flowers cascaded over his head and sifted to the floor. Then the stench of rot unrolled like a blanket.

The source, before something gnawed on it, had been a pigeon. Among poisonous lumps of insulation, where it had dragged itself, the corpse glimmered pearl-grey violet under the baking iron. Charlie scooped it into newspaper and descended.

Down in the garden, where the clothes-hoist spun slowly in the breeze, he retrieved a shovel from the shed. Then, having located the compost heap near the wilderness of poinciana and macadamias, he scraped a hollow, and pushed the pigeon into the soft, busy soil.

Charlie knew more about memorials and vigils than funerals. But the bird had not died easily. Shamefaced, he rested his hand on the parcel, not thinking of the humming green rot within, and said, "Sleep well, mate."

The newspaper folds rasped, as if the corpse had kicked.

Charlie stumbled back, and the bundle did not move again. The pigeon had definitely been dead. Charlie recognised death when he saw it.

After Ida Wren left 21 Volney Street for the last time, the taxi driver had forbidden his daughter to visit. But he was working, and it was a *welcoming* sort of day, so she was halfway over the gate, long toes clenched through the curled iron, when Mr Wren rounded the house.

He wasn't a very memorable-looking person, but enough like Ida that she didn't doubt who he was.

"Hey!" he shouted. The birds on the roof billowed up, shouting too.

"Hey yourself," the taxi driver's daughter said, tightening her hold on the scrollwork. She blew her raggedly cut hair out of her face, and hoped she sounded fearless.

Mr Wren was older than some of her teachers, taller and unshaven. But he still looked as if he disliked kids. Not that *that* mattered—she was in high school now. Besides, this year she'd grown nearly as tall as her mum had been, and she refused to be frightened by people just because they could loom.

He strode to the steps and lifted the plastic bag on the lowest. "Did you leave this?"

"If it's mandarines, they're from Mrs Braithe," she said. She swung her other leg over the gate.

"No!" said Mr Wren, as if she were a dog. "No visitors. No mandarines. My aunt's dead."

"I *know*. I'm going round the back." She dropped into the yard.

"No, you're not," said Mr Wren. He walked sideways up the steps, pointing at her with the bag of fruit. "This is my house."

A hot breeze ruffled through the grass, and an insect stung her ankle. She stood on one leg to scratch.

"You should be in school," he added from the top and then, maliciously, "You should be in uniform."

She was wearing a baggy t-shirt and shorts, and for a moment she panicked—had she forgotten the date? Something bit her again, harder, and she swapped legs. "It's holidays," she said, scornful. "If you heard the bell, they forget to turn it off sometimes, but I don't go to the *primary* school anymore."

Mr Wren retreated through the lattice door. "I bet your parents don't know you're here," he said.

"That's creepy."

"It was a threat!" He'd turned red across the top of his nose.

"My mum's dead!" she yelled. Mr Wren winced, and she added, "I bet you don't know who my dad *is*!" Her dad had driven Ida everywhere, and hadn't even charged. (And if he found out she was here, he'd threaten to send her to her aunt. Mr Wren didn't need to know that.)

"You're a kid!" said Mr Wren. "You shouldn't hang around strangers' houses."

"I'm not!" she said. "I know—knew—Ida."

Mr Wren pinched the bridge of his nose, grimaced, and wiped his fingers on his shirt. "Look," he said, exaggeratedly patient. "It's best if you leave. You—"

A ripple of birdsong. Both glanced up. On the gutter, magpies shuffled, eyes golden red, beaks sharp and blue.

She refused to give in. "I left an assignment in Ida's shed."

"What?" demanded Mr Wren.

"Art." She edged forward and caught her arm on a coil of jasmine. "Famous local people. I'll be really quick."

"No," said Mr Wren, flatly. The birds crowded forward. She stopped as if someone had flung an arm in front of her.

But, satisfyingly, Mr Wren caved first. "I'm cleaning out," he said. "I'll put the art outside the gate if I find it. Okay?"

She wanted to insist—Mr Wren owed her for the welcome gift. She'd seen Mr Braithe and Mrs Tepping bring their offerings, and it had seemed obscurely right to leave something, even just science homework she'd given up on. And the Wrens were the only neighbours who'd given her family anything.

She had, however, a healthy respect for magpies, and for whatever creatures in the grass, busy about her shins, were intent on driving her back.

"Ida never minded," she grumbled, and climbed back over the gate.

◆

Charlie had thought she was Liddy.

The girl—lanky, narrow-faced, her dark hair cropped short—looked nothing like Liddy. But she'd grinned into the sun in exactly the way Ida and Cora once despised.

And Charlie, who barely considered himself an adult, was abruptly aware of every year he'd let slide by.

That shook him more than the pigeon had.

Back inside, filling boxes with the crushed formworks for unmade sculptures, he wondered about his aunt's interest in the girl, and what the girl was telling her father, and what he'd say to Charlie, or the police. Better to be harsh than let someone think he was encouraging kids to roam the yard.

By evening, stiff and sneezing, he'd achieved only a clearer path to the parlour. (Alli would have told him to be ruthless; Liddy would have mocked him for staying indoors and even trying.)

There weren't going to be enough boxes. He was determined not to ask Cora for help, but—hadn't he left a bicycle under the house?

❧

Twilight blew through the high space beneath the floor. Behind slatted bundles of verandah blinds, he found the bicycle, a cobwebbed milk crate still lashed to the rear rack. In it was a bag of mouldering books, including for some reason the pocket poisons handbook he remembered from Ida's first-aid kit. The bike, oversized for him as a boy, was too small, the brakes were disconnected, and the tyres—although somehow unperished—flat.

He wheeled it through grass and dandelions, ignoring the spinning clothesline's thin note, the pigeon's grave-mound. The evening was damp. A fruit bat swung in the trees. Somewhere a dog barked—the first sound Charlie had noticed from beyond the garden.

He propped the bicycle against the shed, beside the shovel. Inside, something flopped scurrying across the floor. He opened the door, and came face-to-face with a person.

With the habit of dreams, Charlie almost seized its throat. Then he realised it was the girl's art project—a papier-mâché bust on a bench, grinning skull-pale.

He touched it, and winced at its lumpish features, the cicada-fragility, an indefinable familiarity. It rocked, knocking hollowly. Perhaps a morbid streak was why Ida had tolerated the girl.

"You," he told it, voice steady, "can stay out here." He'd put it by the gate in the morning. Besides, what if a neighbour glanced over a tall side fence and saw Charlie Wren first burying something, then carrying a mannequin?

The repair kit could wait. Charlie stowed the bicycle under the back steps, and went indoors.

The Third Day

DECOYS

Last century, says Edith Tepping severely, a number of children vanished along the creek.

Some fools, meaning well, made decoy children of hay and stakes and old clothes. They propped the figures in the trees and waited to see what they'd lure.

Long days and nights they watched for predators. What arrived was the mother of the first vanished child. Each evening, she walked down to look closely at the decoys; in the mornings she bent her head as if listening for a voice. Then she took one home.

She planted it in her yard, knee-deep in nasturtiums. While its clothes rotted and its straw seeded, she sang to it, and read, and smiled as if it spoke back.

One by one, the other parents visited the creek. They too chose scarecrows, and took them home to grow in pots, or soften in gardens, or rustle full of spiders on verandahs.

Those neighbours on guard along the bank began to dislike the walk to their own houses, past streets of silent children and contented families. Until the strangling arms of vines, the soft caress of moss, the shrouds of water-wrack enfolded the remaining decoys, they preferred to stay by the creek. They sat close together, eyeing the lengthening shadows of those figures who were never claimed.

CHAPTER SIX

Grace

Grace arrived the next day.

⚜

Charlie dreamed the creek was rising, and half woke to rippling darkness. Cautiously, he lowered one foot to the floor. The boards were dry. Light threaded between the planks, but the water was away downhill, where it should be.

Then headlights kaleidoscoped across his face, broken by leaves and glass. A car turning at the top of the street. Police, perhaps. Charlie was too dazed to deal with that—half asleep, he willed them away, then sank again through layers of roiling decay, distorted reflections, the dead bird struggling, until his fingers pushed *through* it, into earth, and he woke with the smell of dirt in his throat.

Charlie, despite his distaste for living alone, did not turn on Ida's radio. Since his friend Micah's death, he'd stopped listening to the news, in case another murder he'd dreamed proved true. If no deaths were confirmed, he could promise himself he'd run into those lost acquaintances (as Cora, meaning to be kind, called them) in a hostel or bar in a new city. A new life.

The sun was already biting, so Charlie spent the morning in the study, appreciating the dryness of junk mail and bills, council notices and flyers asking "Have you seen this cat?" and hacked-about magazines. He emptied expanding folders pocket by pocket, in case he missed a document Cora wanted to review. At least there were no silverfish, no cockroaches. Not even spiders—elsewhere in Gowburgh, they would have galloped under cabinets, retracted long legs behind frames.

Then he heard a dog *cough*.

Charlie spun around. The noise had been paper falling onto cardboard. A sinkhole of leaflets and forms slithered into new drifts, scrawled with light broken by patterned panes.

⁂

The taxi driver's daughter lived in a brick house, much newer than number 21 (although it felt old to her). It had been built in a decade of hairy carpets and startling wallpaper and kitchens with tiles the colour of meat, and none of her father's efforts could hide that. The windows along the front, over the carport, stretched from ceiling to floor. They were clear on top, like normal windows. But below the central aluminium band, where other houses would have had a wall, there was a wide, cheap, marmalade-orange pane.

The girl lay on her stomach in front of the barley-sugar glass, on the red shag-pile. She had a book between her elbows in case her father, vacuuming the taxi below, decided she was bored and should be filling boxes. But she saw when the creek-person stumbled into Volney Street.

It was not the Witch (who wasn't one, her father said,

just a lady who lived rough and must be left alone), but wore a dress, so the girl assumed it was a woman. She was filthy. Leaves matted her hair, mud crackled her arms, and she lurched to their driveway as if dragged. There, she swayed and stopped.

The taxi driver turned off the vacuum. "Miss?" he hazarded.

His daughter wondered if he recognised the dress. It had belonged to her mother, and ages ago (when, like her mother, she still believed in witches who might bring dead people home) the girl had left it in the ruins by the creek as a gift—an exchange. She knew, now, that the bricks were only the foundations of a washed-away house, and the witch-marks just scratched graffiti. And this wasn't her mother.

The woman said one word. The taxi driver pointed along the street, and she swung away, walking as if on knives. As if the road was hot.

The girl knocked on the glass, and her father glanced up. "Not our problem," he said grimly. "Stay home. Pack your room. Be good."

She nodded, and didn't complain that the house smelled too much of fresh paint, or that there wasn't any *point*, since she wasn't going. In a pinch, she'd run away and camp by the creek in a hut of sticks. When her father drove off, she closed the book and squinted sideways through the window until the woman disappeared.

Out the front door, the girl swung off the steps, over the handrail, and into the cracked concrete yard. She hopped the brick-edged channel of pebbles and snail shells serving as boundary—begun by a previous resident, enlarged by her—then trotted barefoot along the grassy verge, following the grooves left by the postman's motorbike. Occasionally a clammy breeze rose from storm drains and curled around her ankles.

Down in the trees (the girl shivered) you'd have passed the creek-woman without noticing. She was sticks and rags. But she staggered onto the kerb, into the grass, without falling. Her splayed swollen hand trailed through sprays of red honeysuckle, the parchment-scrolls of the white.

If the neighbours saw, they said nothing. After the woman passed, the younger Mr Eising backed his car out, his mouth set. Mr Eising was often disappointed in people.

Edith Tepping, the oldest person on the street, was working in her front garden. Faded among the gerberas and chrysanthemums, she could have seen right down to what was happening, but kept her eyes on the soil.

The creek-woman didn't stop for any of them.

***

The newcomer was trembling by the time she reached number 21. Gazing up through jasmine, its flower-fumes thick in her throat, she let the house slide into place in her mind. It grew, eased, acquired a little more rust, and then had always been in her memory as it was now.

I have been here, she thought. *I, I, I.* Then, furiously, *I am* still *here*.

She curled her hands, stiff and strange, over the gate, and shoved it open.

A tremendous assault of anger, not all her own, shook the sun and the blossoms; the hidden fence kicked against its enveloping foliage. Something not-flowers rushed against her: a *Wren*-ness holding her at bay.

She tore loose from the rage of vines that snared and hooked and spat down white petals. Magpies and butcherbirds—blue knives and scythes of beaks and claws—slashed at her, saw-edged weeds netted her bare feet, sun-hot air snapped at her legs.

But she forced her way up the splintered stairs on hands and knees, wedged her fingers through the lattice door, and shook it.

It did not give. Blow after feathered blow struck at her head, her shoulders, her arms. They were tearing her from herself, cutting and fluttering under her skin, a surging, unkiltering blaze.

With a last effort, she straightened her legs, and surged up in the moment the door was wrenched open.

A man, shouting past her, seized her wrist, hauled her over the threshold, and let her reel, scrambling, to the floor.

Arms over her head, she landed against the wall.

"And stay out!" said the man to the birds, with a finality she didn't recognise. He slammed the door, and they tumbled away, though they could have flown around the lattice, over the balustrade. Daylight silvered his brown hair.

He turned to her, wide-eyed.

And with the same certainty that brought her here—a space in her mind that he belonged in—she was sure he was a Wren.

"Are you—" he began, and stared.

She unfolded, pushing herself to her feet. Raking grazes opened on her mud-crusted limbs; gashes under her matted hair and on her face stretched and gaped.

The Wren said, cautiously, "You'd better come in."

He shepherded her through the house, ran the bath, then returned with clean clothes—soft with age—and fraying towels, and left her. She latched the door with scratched hands and drew a single deliberate breath.

She was inside. Maybe even safe.

And here were new things. Tub. Mirror. Jars and razor. Soap. An unpleasant tumble of slippery fabric on the floor. *For wrapping a corpse in.* The enamel was smooth, the clear hot flow nothing like the creek.

She scrubbed dirt from her wounds and then, submerging, she identified the edges of herself. Here, skin; there, water. *Warmth,* which in the sun she had not realised she was missing. Floating within the shape of herself, she relaxed.

Then, icily, the scratches in her ribs and shoulders widened, and something *not-herself* groped for a way inside.

NO, she shouted, a bubble of a word. She dived to the surface. Waves cascaded over the bathtub's curved rim as she scrambled out, sliding on the wet floor, looking for an attacker to fight.

No one was there.

She wrapped herself in her own arms, the structure of her body sharp against her fingers. The soft edges of abrasions. Twisting, she found herself in the mirror.

Blue smudged her neck and bloomed across her upper back. Bruises, she thought at first—they were little larger than thumbprints. And then, no: *roses.* She had not expected that. But then she would not have known the face reflected over her shoulder, except she had learned its contours from the inside.

"Is everything all right?" the Wren man asked through the door.

"Yes," she lied, and leaned in to study her features, pressed them with her fingertips, seeking shapes she recognised. She pushed closed the pale scratches, until they began to seal; examined her own hands until they made sense as hands.

She dried and dressed gingerly in the clothes he'd given her. The formless dress, vividly patterned, grated against her back, which felt blurred and jagged. Although the clothing, too, was steeped in *Wren*-ness, it blocked the inquisitive air.

She wrung out her hair. Here she was. Alive.

<hr />

Charlie found the first-aid kit where it had always been, still mostly stocked. Then he sat sideways, waiting, on a kitchen chair, one heel on the seat. He rested his chin on his knee, and frowned at his phone.

The house was too porous. He shouldn't have let a stranger in, especially if it was a police matter. But he was so rarely asked to save anyone, and this stranger was so filthy and frantic, the birds so improbably vicious (even for magpies)—he had not thought at all.

How to explain that to Cora? And how to explain to himself his lingering impression of the visitor? The crouching figure had looked wrong, lashing-limbed and bent-angled. Skin dirt grey, blue with flowering tattoos that caught at his memory, pungent with the vegetal reek of swamps. As blank-faced as the model in the shed, swollen handed, with fingers pointed and budding like frangipani branches.

The glimpse had been poisoned by adrenaline. He'd been

expecting, at most, to intercept a delivery of passionfruit or lemons. He'd shouted at the birds as if they'd understand!

He still had not texted Cora when the guest edged into the kitchen. Charlie let his shoulders relax.

She was just a person. Her face was unremarkable, yet it *was* a face. She had pulled Ida's kaftan close, arms tightly folded, but her head was high, and her eyes flickeringly bright.

"Are you . . ." *on drugs* ". . . hurt?" he asked.

She cleared her throat. Charlie pushed away from the chair and fetched a cup of water. She regarded him suspiciously until he sat again.

"I found bandages and antiseptic," he said. He could call an ambulance, or at least a taxi to send her to a doctor. Then he'd have done the right thing and also be rid of her.

The scratches on her face were shallow. Her fingers, grasping her arms, were only fingers, with dirt still under the nails.

Then she opened her hands.

There were splinters in the palms and under the pads of her fingers. The cuts on her arms, although bloodless, were deep. The wrist he had seized was braceleted with his own pale finger-marks.

He found tweezers in the kit, and she removed the slivers herself, swapping hands effortlessly. Charlie, watching, winced.

"Doesn't it hurt?" he demanded at last. She drew her eyebrows together. But when the antiseptic touched the cuts, she hissed conscientiously. Then, carefully, she cleaned and bandaged them, thoughts rippling her bland features.

Finally she said, guarded, "My shoulder." She reached back. "I can't—"

Charlie approached cautiously under her unwavering gaze. Leaf fragments tangled her wet hair, and she smelled of fresh mud, not unpleasant except that he could have pointed to the stretch of creek it came from. The blue tattoos—her one distinct feature—were clustered in a bouquet on one side of her neck. They made it look as if she had been strangled. But her skin was bath-warm and flinched under his hand. Strange as it ever was to touch a living stranger, especially one who smelled like dreams of drownings, he preferred it to touching death.

The kaftan's low neck revealed more small roses, spilling like blood from a cut throat—if blood were blue. They pooled between the tented angles of too-pointed shoulder bones, above a much deeper tear. Improbably deep, separating and fraying as she craned to see. Skin lifted in swollen paperbark layers around a greying fibrous wound.

Not the usual effect of bird claws. Nothing like Ida's anatomical drawings.

"It itches," she volunteered. Itching should mean healing. Then she added, searching for each word, "As if something is scratching to get in."

Charlie awkwardly disinfected the damage and dressed it. If it turned septic or gangrenous, they'd blame him. And yet the Gowburgh of that fear—of doctors and police and hospitals—didn't fit this woman. Like his dreams of murders found and undiscovered, like his sense of waterways (and what they might hold), like all those things he knew better than to talk about, she was implausible. And yet, she was here—a living impossibility. Charlie knew he should be horrified; to his shame, he was pleased. He had been alone a long time among nightmares.

As he pulled the kaftan into place, his fingers grazed the roses. He almost recognised them.

"Who are you?" he asked. "What happened?"

"I don't know."

⋘⟐⋙

She tested his work, guessing how her limbs ought to move, and studied the man leaning against the sink. The intensity that lit him when he pulled her through the door had vanished; he watched her from a long way behind his eyes.

"I woke up by the creek," she said. Speech was growing easier, like vines uncoiling. "I needed to be here. I knew words, the number on the gate. I know *Wren*. Nothing more." Determined to *be,* she'd let go of everything else.

A tide of certainty had pushed her to the house expecting confrontation—her arrival an accusation. Then panicked, she would have clawed her way past, over, through him to save herself, and he might have had any of a dozen faces. If she'd been calm . . . But she knew him now because his was the only face she had seen twice.

He acted so unsurprised that she assumed he knew what must be done. *Perhaps,* she thought, *this is why I came here. Not to fight—to be helped.* It was too easy to feel relief. She had to be careful.

"Ida Wren?" he suggested. "Cora? We're the only Wrens who've lived in the house for years. I'm Charlie."

She shook her head. "Just *Wren*. I don't even have my own name."

"Then what should I call you?"

She wanted to cry *You tell me.* But the idea of herself was so fragile she could not let him choose a name.

She looked at the papers on the table, the map on the wall, its in-wound streets. Names glimmered on it, not entirely new. Bellworth Road. Damson Parade. Grace Avenue. She put her finger there.

"Grace," she said. It meant the least. It would have to do.

***

Charlie asked every question that occurred to him. Nothing flickered in her face. He answered the few she, Grace, knew to ask. The Wrens' history, though long, was not thrilling.

When shadows, deep as the rose-bruises, began to pool under her eyes, Charlie put her in the parlour. He returned with what he had once been given for shock—sweet weak tea, and dry toast—and found her so utterly asleep, he thought she'd died.

His mind skipped ahead. A whole person was different from a pigeon. He imagined the weight of a body, the stairs, the blisters from a shovel. Or waiting for night, and trudging out to the high reeds on the floodplain. He put the mug on the varnished side table.

"Grace." He put his hand in front of her mouth and nose. "*Grace.*"

When he touched her shoulder, she woke like the snap of a rubber band. She seized his shirt before her eyes were open.

Her voice was an indrawn howl.

Charlie forced himself to sound calm. "You weren't breathing."

She drew one deep breath, refocussed, and pushed herself away.

"It would be inconvenient if you stopped," he said. He handed her the crocheted blanket from one of the armchairs.

Rationally, he knew Grace had to recover, if only so the police didn't wonder why Charlie Wren featured in a traumatised woman's history. She must leave, so she didn't trouble Cora's tidy world, or steal Aunt Ida's jewellery, or burn the house down. And something bad had happened to her, or because of her. It was in Charlie's interest to let those problems be solved, to help; to remove the need to tell anyone at all.

All good and sufficient reasons. It didn't matter that he'd recognised her desperation, nor that he selfishly appreciated her unlikely presence, showing no pain, reminding him of waterweeds and survival.

"Sleep," he said. "Then we can talk. Just don't die."

"Don't kill me," she countered, unfolding the blanket.

Charlie, lighthearted with relief, grinned. "I swear it on my life."

She regarded him narrowly, lay back and pulled the blanket over her face.

He ought to warn her not even to pretend to trust him. He ought to worry that she was pulling his impossible dreams of death—of strangers, of friends—into the day.

Grace breathed slowly and ostentatiously on his sofa, pretending to sleep. For the first time in a long time Charlie, as he closed the door and waded through poorly stacked sketchbooks, laughed.

⁂

On the gate of number 21, bronzed by midday sun, the taxi driver's daughter sat side-saddle. She kept her feet outside, but threw twigs into the yard, watching as they arced towards the grass, and were jerked sharply to earth. She frowned at the house. No ambulance arrived, and no one came out.

Finally, she went home.

THE HOUSE
BEHIND THE HOUSE

At school (says a Tepping-Smith nephew, who'd hiked in to Volney Street with beer), Greg and I had to map our block. Our yards backed into each other, but the widths didn't add up. So we went over the fence, and found it: the house behind the house.

It was a little old hut. Silvery gums dropped ribbons of bark on the roof. Inside, the dust was broken by a few clawed prints. The only sound was creaking beams. It was perfect.

We'd say we were visiting each other, then sleep there. We stockpiled mandarines and matches, and yelled when gumnuts clattered on the roof. But I was home the night a storm rolled through, taking out power and stripping branches. After, Greg's mum came for him.

"Greg isn't here," said mine.

"I saw him go over the fence," said his mum. "Before the storm."

I ran to warn him. A tree had crushed the fence, so I scrambled over on its trunk and wound up in Greg's garden. I looked back: our mothers were running out of my house.

"It was right here!" I said. "The yard between our yards!"

But the measurements tallied. Between our chook pen and Greg's trampoline was just space for a fence. After repairs, on either side of its unbroken spine were ordinary yards.

Greg and the mandarines, the matches and the empty windows had vanished forever.

CHAPTER SEVEN

Investigations

Empty, the house had been full of movement. With Grace sleeping, sound seemed absorbed.

Charlie dragged a box of scrapbooks and albums onto the verandah then sat cross-legged, not sorting them. He worried over his thoughts, over Grace's rose tattoo, and the way his mind had recognised its branching, as if he'd traced those flowers once, on someone or something else. The breeze was humid with citrus, the honey-butter scent of gum flowers, the sun-faded sweetness of yesterday-today-tomorrow—it did not calm him.

He had, in the past, tried other means of relaxing, legal and illegal. Cora had disapproved. But fresh air was still precious, and he had little enough control over his life as it was.

Instead, he spun conspiracy theories—Grace as police spy; Grace as a friend of Alli's (had he seen that tattoo at a party?) investigating him. Charlie had no secrets anyone could find. An alibi, however grudgingly given, was another reassuring thing about share houses.

He was glad when Grace came looking for him.

She stood stiffly in the doorway. Her face fit better, but she looked as if she'd been given two black eyes.

"Sleep?" he asked.

She gestured to her shoulder. "The roses."

They had grown.

Charlie, standing, wished he'd counted them before. They'd shed their familiarity and climbed higher on her neck, bled beneath the bandage on her back.

"I feel them," said Grace. "Pressing out. Growing *in*."

He'd camped in enough theatrical households to suspect there were ways to create this effect: petals pushing plush through flesh, thorns reddening as if angled towards the surface. Makeup could mimic the thick dry skin, paler where adhesive pulled at it.

She faced him. "Well?"

Charlie kept his expression neutral. This, for some reason, pleased Grace. Whatever the test, Charlie was passing it.

"Did you—do you—know Alli Kenton?" he asked. It was a chance. Maybe Grace had returned from the place they'd all escaped to, leaving him behind.

Her face did not flicker with guilt or recognition at any of their names. Stef McNally. Jess Poll. Micah Chave.

"They were in the news," he said. "Everyone was searching for them."

"Dead?"

"Disappeared." They were fine, he told himself, although a river taste accompanied their names. No evidence of harm, except to Micah, washing water-bleached under the bridge. No connection between their disappearances, except they had been friends with him.

"And you think I'm—"

"No. The trouble is, people wander off." More, he guessed from his reluctant sense for what passed in the river, than were ever reported. "Someone will be looking for you."

He had not searched for a missing-person report matching Grace—barely possible on his old phone, but not a useful history to have. He steeled himself to make the right decision. Any decision. "I'll call the police. My sister has friends—"

"No," said Grace.

"If you were attacked, if you *escaped*—"

"What if I wasn't?" she replied. "What if I didn't? Suppose *no one* is looking, or someone is but I don't want them to find me? Or what if your sister's friends take me away and I never find out what brought me here?" She shook her head. "I'm going to find answers, and then I'm going to live, Charlie Wren."

She emphasised *Wren* as if he'd inherited some debt to her. He wished he had—he'd have known what to do.

And what (Charlie wondered) if the scratches weren't only from birds? What if the ferocity of her arrival hadn't been fear? What if she had happened to somebody else?

He admired her determination.

"Maybe you'll find something useful." He gestured to the box. "I haven't, but knock yourself out."

Let her steal what she could and leave—Cora wouldn't thank her, but Cora wasn't here. Charlie would be glad of the help.

Still, he decided on a lie. "If you're staying," he began, although Cora had left more than adequate supplies, "we'll need groceries. I'll head to the shops."

~⚬~

There were memories Charlie didn't dwell on, and others that slipped away when he focussed. Bellworth Creek ran through them all.

Descending the street, he sensed floods from the past rising around him. Here knee-deep, now to shoulder, chin. Closing over his head, cold in the heavy sun. The houses glowed white, the sailboat-whirligig among the Eisings' geraniums creaked merrily, but turbulent currents stirred Charlie's hair.

He imagined a faint wake, as if someone else had disturbed this water only he felt. It widened as he went.

Ignore it, he told himself; he wasn't planning on getting into the creek. Cora would say, *It's just the trauma*, gratingly sympathetic, although she'd been hurt worse saving him.

There was a low log fence along the curve where Braithe and Eising joined Volney. Over that, Charlie trod sideways downhill. Woody vines knit trees into a cavern; old bamboo plantings clattered hollowly in its depths.

When he and Liddy practically lived here (Cora less so: two years' difference in age had been a gulf in sophistication), Charlie had learned the names of few trees. Most were weeds—mallow and pepper, tulip trees and potato vine. Escapees from gardens, crowding out hazier identifications: casuarina, quandong, lilly pilly. And last time he'd been among them, accompanied by police, he'd panicked and started choking on air.

The unseen trail widened too much to be useful.

In the corner of an old foundation he found a damp scrap of paper. Written very definitely on it was, "For the Witch. Please bring mum back. Thank you." In his experience, that was not a request that was ever granted. There was no sign of what gift had been left.

Downstream, where the sky opened, cannas nodded and the reeds were starred by spidery lilies. Their stalks curved like a bowerbird's nest, as if something had slept there, but not recently—fresh seedlings were sprouting. The tunnels threading the undergrowth were too small for adults.

The invisible wake had vanished into the visible. Insects dimpled and shirred the tannin surface.

In the other direction, there was still a narrow path, well-trodden although uncomfortably close to the bank. Between mangroves and mulberries an inlet broke it, and he scrambled up the other side, staining his hands crimson on fallen fruit. Coral flowers sparked through the canopy, afterimages of sun.

He remembered this: it had been a road to adventure, and the way to the Drowned House.

⁂

The taxi driver's daughter ducked behind a fallen tree, her fingers threaded among pebbled seeds. She was not allowed to *play* here, but she could pretend this was an investigation.

Mr Wren walked purposefully for someone new to the street. He frowned at what remained of her message to the Witch, and strode into the grey reeds. Other kids—now on holidays without her—said they'd heard groans in there, and seen a puddle that reflected *not your face*. And then hands would reach through the grass and grab your ankles. She had grown too much to believe that, and yet . . .

But Mr Wren, emerging from the reeds, only looked re-signed.

She followed him upstream past the bend where a boy (years and years ago, she'd heard) had been pulled down into the mud to vanish entirely. Her stomach began to crawl, and the back of her neck itched, like it did at the worst of her aunt's fairy tales. She put her hands in her pockets, and found only a squashed roll of mints—nothing that was ever useful in stories. Quiet pressed on her ears like the deep end of a pool.

In the trees, metal clanked mindlessly against metal.

She opened her mouth to call for Mr Wren to wait—and for the first time realised, in a way that felt frighteningly grown-up, that this really wasn't a game.

That meant there was no shame in running home.

⚜

Charlie pushed upstream, taking the path he and Liddy had taken when she'd dared him to creep all the way to the Drowned House.

Uphill, behind hoop pine and bloodwood, were homes and cars, tidy yards. But here a stone-curlew sobbed, subsidences mimicked shallow graves, and with every step he stumbled into legends.

The ruin of a car crouched, grouted with lichen ("There's still a skeleton sitting at the wheel"). A clutch of tractors sank into the soil ("On moonless nights, you can hear their engines . . ."). A horse whinnied on the opposite bank; on his own side was a slithering splash.

The Beast of Bellworth, he thought, amused. *Or was it "the Butcher"?*

The thought sobered him: Charlie Wren, hands stained mulberry red, tramping through the undergrowth.

And he'd found nothing to explain Grace, no sign of a crime of which he should be forewarned. Maybe when he got home she'd have wandered off, confused or drunk. But he recalled the clarity of her stare.

"What are you looking for, Charlie Wren?" he asked himself.

Yet he had not imagined Grace, and she was something surprising. Even, perhaps, marvellous. And if she and her roses were true, then there was a chance the deaths he had imagined, that he'd accidentally discovered—

He usually avoided pressing on old wounds. Life, as Alli pointed out (exhaling smoke and making it sound worthwhile), had to be gotten on with. But the creek, this shifting green, wasn't real life. Certain he was alone, Charlie rested his hand on a file-rough trunk, closed his eyes, and let down his guard.

His feet chilled, his fingers grew cold, and—

There was no chance to reconsider, to leap clear. He was in creek water, in *flood* water, and it was rising. The surface stormed overhead, churned higher, and bright breath threaded upward, vanishing. He was rolled and dragged into the mud under the overhanging bank, into a crowd of deaths innumerable, unnameable, clasping at him with soft and rotting fingers, dragging him into the rich dark earth which filled his mouth his nose his eyes—

Don't die, he'd said to Grace, as if it were easy.

With a final spasm, he clawed into roots and grass, hauled himself through brown darkness. And he could breathe.

Apart from sweat and grass-stains, his clothes were dry. He was on his back, a little off the path, halfway to the house where a man who'd attacked him had lived and been murdered, years ago.

Above, a currawong sang.

His jaw was clenched, his limbs as weak as wrung-out

towels. The light flickered, but that was the between-ness of the creek, and he'd held it at bay.

"What are you're looking for, Charlie Wren?" he asked again.

He was sick and hungry, and had dared enough for one day. There were sufficient wonders at home.

⚬

Sleep benefitted Grace's roses, pliant and springing. Her bones, however, were brittle, her skin flaked. Hard toast and milk-skinned tea rotted in her stomach.

Her one certainty had towed her here, and she did not know how much time was left to find answers.

She stalked through the ticking, settling house. Shook a locked door and peered through the keyhole at a net of muted shadow. Charlie's room, perhaps.

In the kitchen, she peeled a mandarine, but the white webbing around its segments dried her mouth. Instead, she studied the clippings on the refrigerator. Road upgrades diverted around Bellworth, land reclamations narrowly avoided, petitions against developments threatening the suburb's character.

One had a picture of a young woman, her perfect smile softened by newsprint. She shifted, took shape, turned towards Grace, and for a moment—but it was a breeze lifting the paper. Grace held it flat. The woman was clearly related to Charlie, although she stood with shoulders back and chin raised, smart in a plum-coloured jacket and flowered dress.

Grace, conscious now of her own shapeless garment,

searched on, grimacing at features in the fretwork panels above doors, and at the rosy faces in old photographs. Seen together, the family type—a mould from which Charlie had been cast, without significant variation—was distinct: an inherited nose, a recurring Wren chin, here rigid with disapproval. But their disdain was as reassuring as clothes were, and the warm bathwater had briefly been: a boundary between herself and everything else.

She returned to the bathroom and, now wary of the tub, soaked her dry hands in the sink, wiped the nape of her neck, and felt the roses drinking. She worked lotions from the cabinet into the powdery marks on her arms, smoothed the scratches on her face. The relief was slight, and the choking essences of violet and gardenia bullied their way into memory.

And the mirrors in the house, scalloped and frosted, unsettled her. In one annex, by a narrow daybed patchworked with coloured light, Grace saw someone sliding away. She snatched at them, and discovered a mirrored closet door swinging as the house eased.

She confronted her reflection. Draughts through the floorboards lingered over her neck, her jaw. A gaze pressed from the mirror, pushed itself against her face. For a moment air stretched over her mouth, membranous against the shape of a word.

Grace slammed the door shut. Imagination.

On the front verandah, ignored by the birds, she leafed through papers. Photographs of a suburb and a family. A battered old image—fly-specked—of a large formal group on a wide sloping lawn in front of a house with deep verandahs. The house was too small to be this one, but Grace lingered on it. *Wrens, before the flood*, said sepia ink on the back, with a spiderweb of branching and rejoining lines. A family tree.

There were other pictures, newer, of marriages and deaths, advertisements for new estates, invitations to Ladies' Teas. Black-and-white pictures of minor dignitaries, matrons with heavy rings, an aproned man grinning beside a plate-glass butcher's window. He resembled Charlie, better-fed, with sideburns.

She no longer knew which, if any, of these faces she'd already known. But she felt one stab of recognition at a modern photo of children in school uniforms: Charlie, young, with combed-flat hair, next to the girl from the refrigerator—although he was the shorter, they might have been twins. Then another picture: the girl, only a little older, in a red suit. The picture was cut from thin shiny paper: "Bellworth's own Cora Wren." Then news clippings, some about people Charlie had mentioned, most about names she couldn't place.

Grace dug for the next scrapbook. The movement pulled the bandage on her shoulder, and adhesive ripped her skin. It tore towards her neck; fragile as rotten fabric. Air fluttered its edges, picked at the wound.

Grace dropped the book and grabbed behind her. As she twisted, her spine pulled awry, and something in her shoulder folded like a green stem. But her fingers closed on frantic struggling. She dragged her prey around and saw—*nothing*.

The knuckles of her empty hand strained knife-sharp under her skin. And yet—neither translucent nor transparent, but *not there*—an invisible presence fought against her grasp.

Larger than a magpie, smaller than a possum, no more texture than a strong breeze. It twisted, flattening between her fingers like clay, wriggling under her nails, as if to lever them up. It writhed against her palms, burrowing through her pores.

Grace acted as thoughtlessly, as hungrily as when she broke open the mandarine. The absence thrashed between her jaws, convulsed in her throat, and she had swallowed it and there was no chance to change her mind. A shudder of fragmenting vision—a whirling view of the verandah from the wrong angle, the chasms between the floorboards, towering cliffs of grooved walls. A terror too vast for her body, then too tiny, and Grace was herself again.

She lay tumbled over a cane chair in a clutter of shoes and umbrellas. There was a new scrape on her arm, chalky and abraded, red welts on her shins, and a thin retreating chill in her side, as if something were being unspooled.

It was the wire rib of an umbrella. Grace eased it out and clamped her hand over the wound. Numb with revulsion, shoulder grating woodenly, she limped into the bathroom, and examined the puncture. There was only a trickle of pale fluid. Once she had bandaged it, the realisation she had *eaten* the invisible thing rushed in.

She tried to vomit. Not because of the taste—there was none. Nor from dizziness, which had passed (although the world remained canted). Nor was it the sensation; she rinsed her mouth out until that was gone. What shook her was her own willingness—her *instinct*—to destroy.

She bared her teeth in the mirror. They were not pointed, but she had threatened Charlie when he woke her. He said people had disappeared; the unquiet house could hide evidence of her own guilt as easily as any Wren's. Would she lash out again? Had she hurt someone before?

The roses had crawled around her neck, reaching towards

her collarbone, and memory grew with them—this hunger, or an older one.

Grace gripped the sink and told herself the house was getting to her. There was no other life except the new shoot of the plant on the kitchen windowsill—the rest was layered, bloodless histories. She'd end up mummified in drifts of paper, her limbs drying to chalk.

~❧~

Grace opened the back door, gingerly. But no birds attacked, or even eyed her askance. She descended, sat on the last step, and sank her feet into the grass. *I could grow down into this earth,* part of her thought. She made herself breathe, like an ordinary person. Like Charlie. In. Out. The hole in her side leaked air.

The breeze was damp, without ulterior motive, spiced by no memory except the nasturtiums' peppery glow. The sunlight, deepening gold, was sculpted only by leaves. Grace was herself (*a* self, singular) again. As if—as if she had eaten.

She forced her attention into the yard. Past the nebulous familiarity of it, flat as a photograph. The more she looked, the longer she realised it was. What seemed a backdrop to shed and clothesline was merely the first layer. Behind it, tree-tunnels receded, and the richness of old soil and new growth deepened as silently as the thought, *I know this.*

Near, the stake of an old trellis tilted sideways, its ties cracked with age.

Recognising the garden was good. It meant her past was growing.

The section of trellis leaned again.

Grace's gaze snapped to it. Three long slats, human-height, were tied together by weathered cords and dead vines. A paste of dried leaves, partially skinned with shredded possum fur, plastered the join, wrinkling as it shifted.

Just the breeze, she told herself, as dust flecked from the rigid tripod. Then grey tendrils unravelled towards her, and broke into fingernail-crescents, and the whole arrangement stilt-stalked forward.

Grace rose. There was no weapon near. Although this thing was visible, she refused to believe that the world held not simply creatures and trees, but things in between.

She clenched her fists. "Get. Away." She needed to resist leaping with teeth and claws. But she would, if she had to.

Another stick twitched forward, splintering.

Grace stood her ground. This long-legged marionette did not frighten her as much as she had already frightened herself.

Then it tripped, clattered sideways, and lay twitching. Grace laughed with relief.

The tremors grew faster, uncontrolled, as if the thing was being violently shaken. The fur ruffled, dented, flattened as jaws would have flattened it—if there had been jaws to see. Leaves shredded from the brittle covering and were flung aside. The timber snapped into kindling.

Grace scrambled up the stairs and slammed the door behind her.

The attacker—low to the ground, ferociously strong—was invisible, but Grace had seen enough. The scarecrow, or whatever it was, was being ripped apart.

⚬

Charlie climbed Volney Street, mulberry-stained hands in his pockets, head bent. He ignored the sunlight's last mustard-yellow spill, the thin warnings of wind chimes. The Drowned House squatted in his mind.

Once, he and Liddy had been fascinated by the old man there—Bill Volney, unwashed and angry and regarded superstitiously by the neighbours. Liddy invented histories: he'd escaped a giant shark and now stayed near shallow water; he was an evil sorcerer, an archaeologist hiding from an ancient curse, a murderer on the run . . .

The house, however, was not an invention—that was the problem. Built outside the boundary of Bellworth (*no suburb will claim it, and the maps leave it out*), it had been flooded and never cleared. And in the creek, the old man had once tried to kill Charlie. Both Wrens had scars to prove it.

But when Charlie reached home (Ida's place, he corrected himself), for a moment he forgot the Drowned House. Jasmine clouded the gate, and all the coloured windows were lit from within.

The Fourth Day

HOUSEMATE

My first share house was on Bellworth Road (says a refugee from flooded Braithe Street). I found my housemate—a vet student—through friends of friends.

It was typical: high-set, carpets so thin the winter wind stripped the heat out through your soles. We had the furniture that cycles through every student house in Gowburgh, and a gloriously ugly vase I found in an op-shop the day I got the lease.

One day the police came by to see me about . . . something. They acted strange, and I blamed it on the decor that comes with a vet student: a cat skull on top of the television; arm-length rubber gloves draped over a door; a snake in its tank on the coffee table. My housemate stayed in her room, and I apologised for her, as you do. After I saw the police out, I looked around with fresh eyes, expecting to see more oddities and start laughing.

But the house was half empty. All my housemate's furniture, including our horrible couch and three chairs, was vanished. So were the gloves, the cat skull, the snake, the frozen mice in the freezer—and her. Evaporated, as if she'd never lived there.

I had to move—I couldn't get anyone new in time for the rent. She was the most conscientious person I ever lived with, in that regard: her share of the money always on time, neatly stacked in cash under the awful vase in the kitchen.

CHAPTER EIGHT

Old Friends

Although the lights were on when Charlie returned, Grace was in the parlour, a chair against the door. Charlie eased it open enough to peer in and glimpse Grace asleep, and books scattered on the floor. But he'd learned not to wake her.

In the kitchen, he rinsed away a froth of green foam around the drain, then washed his stained hands and went for the bread, but it was already blossoming with mould. He rummaged in the refrigerator, instead—it didn't look like Grace had touched the food, so maybe she wouldn't notice he hadn't brought any groceries back.

While he ate he searched on his old phone, with difficulty, for anything explaining her roses. Even, despite misgivings, for missing persons. Compressed and pixelated, the pictures showed him faces he already knew a little too well. He distracted himself by emptying the wardrobe in the annex.

Ida had thrown out everything of Charlie's; no evidence remained that he'd ever lived in the house. But bundled in with shoes and racquets was a street directory as old as he was. He looked up Bellworth, its creek narrowing upstream to Greenstone, and fell asleep trying to make the outlines match his memories.

⟡

Midmorning—after Charlie had found the bicycle pump, filled the tyres, turned slow circles around the washing line, and exhausted his knowledge of bicycle repair—he checked on Grace again. She was seated, now, staring into the fireplace. The encyclopaedias were loose around her feet.

"Come in," she said, immobile.

Charlie put his shoulder to the door. The chair bracing it caught in the carpet, then crashed over. He righted it hastily. Grace hadn't turned.

How are you? Did you remember more? Why the chair? Why every light?

"Did you find anything in those?" he asked.

"No," said Grace through her teeth. "Pressed flowers."

"How are the roses?"

By way of answer, Grace slowly bent her head to let him see. The lamp, swaying, made her skull look the wrong shape. Blue flowers, grown larger, climbed into her hair and spilled over her shoulder.

On her back, below the brash print of Ida's dress, that first wound had spread and torn. Its grey fibres frayed like palm matting. Underneath, instead of veins or muscle, was a net of blue-green vines. The colours reminded him of the pigeon, and the way it pulled apart—

He didn't know how Grace wasn't dead. But she'd fought her way here and, tense beneath his examination, still held herself together. Charlie, although queasy, admired that.

He could still let himself panic—call for help, or let Cora make arrangements. Yet if this infection, and possibly

Grace herself, did not belong to that orderly world, why should the solution?

"It isn't good, is it?" she said, calmly.

He'd follow her lead. "I have an idea," said Charlie, and left the room.

⚜

Grace, frantic, wanted to pursue him, but she was lashed together by vines, dried into position, defenceless. She stared down at books which held only common plants: oleander, lilies, lantana. They were as desiccated as her bones and nails, powdery as her skin.

By the time Charlie returned, carrying a lidded basket, Grace had adjusted her position. Joint by joint, she forced her limbs into place, gripped the sofa's arm and forced herself to her feet. Things snapped and tore in her back. She wanted to weep with frustration, but no tears came. At least it would be difficult for her to hurt anything—anyone.

"I was looking for string," he explained, coldly offhanded. "I don't think Aunt Ida ever used this. A dried-up mouse was curled around the pincushion. Overlooked, not eaten." She didn't know why he'd add that.

He produced a long needle and a spool of heavy thread, and squinted as he threaded it. His hand shook.

"What are you doing?" she grated.

"You're fighting to stay upright," he said. "If we can tie everything together—the vines, and the . . ."

"Bones?" she suggested. (Not bones. Too light, too yielding.)

"—maybe you'll have a chance to heal."

"You're a terrible liar," Grace said.

"Yes," said Charlie. She resented his grin, but was relieved by it.

Since she could barely raise her arms, he cut the back of the dress. "I haven't started on my aunt's room," he said. "You can have any clothes you find in there. I should probably run the needle through a flame or something, though I'm not technically giving you stitches. Are you sure you want me to do this?"

"It's your idea." Her voice caught. When she coughed, fibres in her unravelled.

"Tell me if it hurts," said Charlie. She felt him anchor the thread to something below her shoulder blade, pull and knot it to another branching structure, lace that to a third. Her bones bent like cane, hooped into shape, pulling her upright with them. Even when he tacked and knotted the fraying layers of her skin down over the crossed threads, it did not hurt.

It was a new experience, wholly her own. Too many of those and—supposing she held together—she'd never find her way back to who she'd been.

"This isn't natural, is it?" she said, in case she knew less about the world than she thought.

"Stranger things happen," said Charlie. Listening for a lie, she heard strain in his voice. "I'm using as much willpower as thread here, Grace, but I *think* this will hold until—"

"Until what?"

"Instead of the shops, I went to the creek yesterday," he confessed, testing a knot. One of her shoulders pulled sharply. She braced her hands on the sofa. Had he doubted her story? Did she have something to hide?

"The creek nearly got me, when I was a kid," he said. "A

man lived upstream. Kids said he was a—that he knew all sorts of things. Superstition, or too many horror movies. Anyway, he's gone, but the path to his place is being used, and someone's been leaving out wishes."

She heard the scissors and then Charlie moved around to face her. "Grace, I don't believe in, well, magic. But no, none of this is natural."

The witch. The word glimmered from a waking memory. "You don't mean just me," she said.

"It can't hurt to go *see*, can it? Come with me. I'll find you some shoes—"

"I don't want to go," said Grace, hastily. Let him answer his own questions—he didn't need to know she could scarcely stand. Then, because he looked puzzled, she added, "Something I ate disagreed with me."

⁂

On the creek path, more had changed than the light.

The Charles Wren who turned home yesterday was now tree-shadows. Today, Charlie was—unsettlingly—elated. It was easy to hold himself clear of the water's grasp, if only by means of new memories: Grace's spine, its gnarled spikes pushing through sliding hanks of tendons; thorns tearing leaf-mould skin. Long fresh bruises, already blue, and Charlie's hands actually inside her back, clumsily binding snapped twigs.

He had *done* something, as practical as improbable. He had a plan, however little sense it made. And he wanted to believe that since Grace existed at all, she could survive . . .

Past where he had fallen, a shattered fence foundered

under flood-wrack. It looked like a creature weighted by matted fleece. On the other side—

People.

No. Stooks of branches, grotesquely lichened. Tree guards from an abandoned planting.

He stepped over the swaybacked fence.

Mosquitoes whined thickly in the steaming air, but the birds had stopped singing. The farther he walked, the more human the figures became, glimpsed from the corner of an eye.

The resemblance vanished when he examined one closely: twigs and the beaded white stems of palm-fruit, thatched by rotting grass. In its hollow chest, a mud-wasp nest clotted into a heart. A necklace of tiny amber beads, dirt-crusted, hung inside the head-shaped cage. But no skin. No roses.

He went on, and the well-trodden path between gum trees and splintered basketworks was far, far longer than it had been—

The path ended at a greenly stagnant stretch of creek, plucked and dimpled by insects. A temporary causeway of drums and planks broke its oily surface—surely not the same bridge he remembered.

("The car yards in Greenstone have poisoned the water so much, your reflection will come right out of it and *grab you by the ankles.*" Liddy's voice, daring him over.)

The first crate dropped sluggishly under his weight. Charlie, immersed in the creek's miasma this whole way, supposed falling could be worse only by a matter of degrees. Nevertheless, as he crossed, he kept his gaze high for fear of seeing anything below.

Then he scrambled between vines into a feather-reeded paddock. On a rise at its heart, curtained by casuarinas and hibiscus, orphaned of any roads, was the Drowned House.

Younger than number 21, it was a dense two-story house of asbestos boards (although lead-lit windows, dust-flattened, marched along one upper wall), with diseased concrete stairs running up one side. The old man had died out here. The morning he was discovered, Cora, pale from her own injury, had relayed the news, glowing at saving Charlie *again*—this time from nightmares. But Charlie had already dreamed of too many feet fording the shallow crossing, trailing mud through the reeds. He'd woken to the taste of blood.

Now the house brooded over an accretion of garbage, flooded and thrown out and dried and soaked again. A path was worn in the grass beside it, and from beyond he heard faint chimes.

No other sound—not a tidal roar drifting from the highway, nor the lawnmower-buzz of a plane scudding overhead in the teeth of the breeze.

Charlie picked his way through unnameable trash to a mould-blackened wall, and peered into a downstairs window. The frame was webbed with dirt. A mash of paper and cloth plastered the pane. Inside, like a swirl of smoke, he imagined the after-echo of rushing water, but outside all was still.

"Charlie *Wren*?" said a voice.

He tripped as he turned. Behind, like a loss dredged from the creek, stood a woman laden with bags. An old woman, he thought first, her hair reddish grey and her clothes draggled.

The Witch from the letter, he thought next, weathered but not so very old.

Then he looked at her again, and said, "Liddy?"

⁓

She didn't take him past the uninhabitable house, to wherever the chimes were hung, to where—he supposed later—she must live. Instead, she dropped her bags, assessed his height, seemed disgusted, and climbed to sit on the steps above him, elbows on knees. No one except Cora had ever successfully looked down on Liddy.

"Where have you been?" he said, waving aside a cloud of insects. "When did you come home? Does anyone know you're here?"

"Of course they do."

"Does Cora?" It was out of his mouth before he realised Cora would have told him.

"I didn't feel the need to attract her notice," said Liddy, drily.

A large dog, shadow-striped, padded up and reclined on the ground between them. Liddy, whom Ida accused of spoiling Dennis, had always wanted a dog. But that Liddy—round-faced, sturdy, and sunburnt—had run away. Now her features were lined and her big hands blunt-fingered, and she was with him.

"Why are you back?" she asked.

"Aunt Ida died. I'm packing her things. Liddy—"

She raised her eyebrows. "Is Cora helping?"

"She's busy," said Charlie, slapping a mosquito.

"Isn't she always. Why are *you* bothering me?" When he

hesitated, she jerked her chin to the place where the dog lolled. "Old Bill died there."

Charlie felt no malevolent presence. Just sadness, flood-marks, his own bewilderment. The dog panted around large teeth.

"I heard there was a witch," he said, hoping she'd roll her eyes, come down from her stairs, and explain where she'd been. Why she'd left him behind.

"I'm no witch."

"You're not getting bitten."

She didn't smile. "I've been here too long. A big sacrifice for a small power."

He didn't ask how long; he was afraid he knew, and at home, Grace was falling apart.

"A friend was hurt in the creek, and doesn't remember what happened. I thought—"

She cocked her head. "The wrong person would be blamed?"

Charlie's face heated. "She's getting worse," he said. "She's . . ." Liddy might laugh, but Liddy always had. "She's decaying."

"That's a problem that'll fix itself," said Liddy. "Throw her into the scrub and leave her. She wouldn't be the first."

"I *know*!" said Charlie, fourteen again and easily baited. "I dream about it. Drownings and murders. " Death stain-ing his arms.

"Poor Charlie," said Liddy, with none of Cora's kind-ness. She hadn't been talking about Alli or the others.

"I didn't forget you!" he protested. "You ran away." And he'd missed her like she'd been cut out of him. But that was half their lives ago.

"Yet here I am," said Liddy. She stopped his apology

with a slash of her hand. "Forget it. Pretend you're here to see a witch."

"You aren't one."

"That doesn't stop people wanting things. Why would you be different?"

Charlie swallowed the sting. He was here—a short walk, a long fall into the past—for Grace's sake. At least if Liddy disbelieved him, she'd be honest.

He told her about Grace. The roses. The skeleton-leaf layers under her skin where there should have been flesh.

Liddy said, "Is that all?"

They were outside time, and this was Liddy. "She came from the creek," said Charlie. "And Liddy, you left before I could tell you, but ever since my—my accident, I've been able to sense the water." Able, with effort, to block out what drifted in it. It was a relief to tell her—she was the one person apart from Cora he would have told, if she'd bothered to stay until he'd recovered.

"People do," said Liddy, sourly.

"No, I mean—I can tell you where floods have been, what's in the currents. And sometimes if I'm not careful I know where the dead wash ashore. I've dreamed of corpses before they were found." Before they were missed.

"Grace is part of that," he went on. "And I didn't have anywhere to start for answers, except the stories about the Drowned House, and secrets. I want to fix things, Liddy. Or at least not make them worse."

Liddy gazed down, considering.

"Grace doesn't want to die," he said.

"I'm sorry for her, but it doesn't make her special. She picked the wrong rescuer."

Charlie lost his temper. "You left me, Liddy! You didn't even say goodbye!"

"You wouldn't let me in!"

"I was sick! They didn't let me see anyone!"

The dog growled; thunder rippled its brindled fur.

Charlie and Liddy glared at each other until the animal settled, biting at its own shoulder.

"Fine!" said Liddy at last. "*You* know people drown. But traffic with the creek isn't one way. Sometimes things come back. Things, not people."

"But—"

She held up her hand. "It's worse lately. A blocked drain, the start of a flood. Deaths are damming up, overflowing. Have you felt that?"

"No," lied Charlie.

Liddy looked like she knew. "It's worse lately. Especially since Ida. Did she die in the house?"

"In hospital."

"Hmm," said Liddy, and shook a thought away like a bug. "I keep clear of Volney Street, but your neighbours aren't sleeping well. Old Mrs Braithe came to me the other week. She's afraid—*Mrs Braithe,* Charlie! Not of dying: of not being able to."

(The dead pigeon, kicking as he buried it.)

"What about Grace?" he said. "She's a person, not a thing, and she's getting worse."

"You used to give up faster," said Liddy. "Listen, most stories I'm told don't happen twice. But I'll tell you three things I've heard, and maybe the answer will be in front of your nose this time, too."

"I didn't know you were here," said Charlie.

Liddy counted on her fingers. "One. An infection. A

man cuts his hand, say, and a plant, or something a plant remembers being, gets inside. Gets comfortable. If he yanks it up by the roots early, cuts it out, he'll be fine. Leave it, and it gets into liver or heart, starts getting *ideas*. There's no good ending. That's science."

She fixed a glare on him, and he stayed silent. "Two. Sometimes memories stick around, if they haven't worked out they're dead. Those don't learn, or change. I've heard a trick is to show them their own headstone, or an empty mirror."

"And three?" said Charlie, still hoping for a sensible solution. And Grace must have seen herself in the bathroom mirror.

"Three: You get hollow spots—an eggshell, a tangle of grass, a loneliness. It's nest-shaped, so something climbs into it. People have made themselves bad problems that way."

"Like the scarecrows in the trees?"

"They stay put," said Liddy. "Nests aren't for walking around in."

But Grace was alive, and there was no such thing as her blue roses.

"Of course," added Liddy, "sometimes things *pretend* to be people."

Grace was too determined to be pretending.

"And that's all?"

"All I know." Liddy stood up briskly. The dog sat up, yellow gaze fixed on her. "Go," she commanded.

Charlie lingered. "If you need anything . . ."

"Nothing you have," said Liddy. "I've looked after myself right here for a long time." But as he reached the creek, she called, "I hope *you* at least got to see the world."

The breeze had fallen, although bells still rang behind the Drowned House. Charlie crossed the creek, imagining thoughts fluttering moth-soft against his, and trudged home through the tunnel of fig and tea trees.

He forced himself not to shy away from Liddy's anger. She'd never left—she'd been over the creek the whole time. She'd believed he knew and didn't care. Worse, he *should* have found her. Instead—what? He'd spent fourteen years being merely Charlie Wren, who was almost murdered. Too vague to be ambitious, not precisely unreliable, but for whom allowances were made. Charles Matthew Wren, whom even the police only half suspected.

But Grace wasn't dead, wasn't a memory, was held together by a plant that didn't exist. Whether she was a monster, or proof Charlie wasn't one, she had come up from the same creek fighting.

Charlie envied her.

BOUGAINVILLEA

This was one farm (says Edith Tepping, as if time began then).
Outbuildings, cemetery, stockyards, tennis court. They moved the
house uphill after a flood, but when the jacarandas bloom—as
often as not, now—you see an avenue of purple: the road to the
old foundations. A bit of the citrus orchard is on Eising Street.
And partway to the creek was an enormous scarlet bougainvillea.

After subdivision, that lot was levelled. A family built
there—not our sort of people, although my grandmother (who
was young) was fond of them. But their house rustled, *like*
branches with a honeyeater in them. When the curtains were
still, shadow flowers swayed on the walls.

The new owners aged quickly, veins dark in swollen limbs.
The house decayed, its white paint green with algae. Their son
dreamed of papery blossoms and smelled, my grandmother said,
of dry flowers. When she was sent on a visit home to England,
he waved goodbye between branches of bougainvillea, and she
thought leaves fell from his lips.

She returned a year later, chic and worldly, and a new house
stood where his had been. "What happened to the house before
that house?" she asked.

There never was one, she was told. Only a grand crimson
bougainvillea, as much as seventy years old. It took five men to
dig the roots out. And such things they found beneath . . .

CHAPTER NINE

Cora

Mr Wren was out. The taxi driver's daughter crumbled bread over the gate of number 21 and whistled through her teeth. Whatever had bitten her legs the day before and snatched at the falling twigs hadn't been insects; there were no red lumps, only faint curved bruises. Today, she watched for ripples in the grass.

"Hello, young lady!" said a bright voice behind.

The girl dropped the bread and whipped around.

She knew Miss Wren by sight: entering or leaving number 21, in photos on brochures, giving a speech to senior students. Occasionally, on the news, Miss Wren stood near the official speaking at press conferences. Her mother had been impressed: "Such a young woman, and so successful."

Up close, Miss Wren was far shorter than her brother, and *pretty*. Under her cropped red jacket, her flowery dress flared too much for a teacher or a real estate agent. Her hair was caramel-thick and glossy as lacquered paper, and she looked as if she was going to a wedding, or—apart from the scuffed shoebox under one arm—like the fancier sort of librarian. She wore Ida Wren's pearls.

"Your father drove Ida," said Miss Wren. "So kind. Are you waiting for someone?"

The taxi driver's daughter was conscious, as she had not been when she dressed, that her t-shirt was full of holes and her shorts streaked with paint, and that her hair had been cut by her father.

"Ghosts!" she said, panicked. "Dog ghost. Maybe."

"Ghosts!" exclaimed Cora, her voice warm and her eyes dancing. "And you're feeding them. What a clever idea."

The girl, humiliated by praise, thought miserably, *She is wonderful, though.*

"Come in," said Cora. "People have written about this house, but it still has secrets—anything might be hidden in a wall, or stored underneath. I bet you'd find spirits if you searched."

"Mr Wren told me to stay out," said the girl in a rush. She felt a push, now, whenever she leaned over the gate. And she was too shy to say she hadn't noticed any hauntings when Ida let her in, or to ask Cora any of her many questions.

"Oh dear," said Cora. "Poor Charlie isn't good with people. *I* say you can visit any time. But today, you'll have to let me by."

The taxi driver's daughter skipped aside as smartly as if Miss Wren's pinkly manicured hands had lifted her clear.

Cora, gleaming and important, went in, and a surge of dissatisfaction overturned the girl's awe. It wasn't fair that Miss Wren was like that, while other people were scruffily angular, and embarrassed, and unable to lure out even a grumpy breeze.

Grace refused to stiffen into immobility. She forced herself to keep moving, to taste a spoonful of honey—the sweetness buzzed in her skull.

In the bathroom, where a ring of green stained the basin, she soothed her coarsening skin again. Then she staggered from room to room, looking for what had brought her here.

Charlie's aunt Ida's room was a rayon-and-talcum cavern lined with wardrobes, each filled to capacity then abandoned. Grace studied several formal photos—a sternly glamorous woman who aged across them, turning towards Grace like the photo on the refrigerator, shrinking in on herself. "Do I know you?" asked Grace. The only movement was her own reflection in a dust-fogged mirror, curtained by costume jewellery. On the wall beneath, a little block of wood sat across the gap between two boards. Grace twisted it, and a door swung open on shrill hinges.

It did not lead to the locked room, but to a windowless space between rooms, braced by beams. The air stung of . . . Grace did not know where she had last encountered *camphor*, but the word sat unmoored in her mind. And here were more bags and hangers and swags of fabric. Charlie would not be pleased, and Grace grinned. But it was narrow and dark, and something rustled behind the walls. She hooked an armful of clothes and backed out.

She was wrestling with the buttons on a shirt when the kitchen screen clattered, and light footsteps struck the linoleum floor.

Grace had not heard the bells on the lattice, or the front door, but the steps were brisk. Good news. She emerged, pushing up her new sleeves, and at the kitchen door said, "Charlie?" as another voice said the same thing.

⁂

Cora Wren, off the articles, out of the photos, was drying her hands on a pineapple-patterned tea towel. She was bright as geraniums, and so self-possessed there was hardly a pause before her expression warmed into a smile.

"I don't believe we've met," she said, neatening the towel. Her lipstick was vivid—Grace could taste the wax of it on the air. "I'm Cora."

"Grace," said Grace.

Cora, shorter than Grace, looked both exactly and nothing like Charlie. Her cherry-red shoes snapped smartly on the floor, and she clasped Grace's rough fingers—Ida's hand cream had evaporated already—in her cool ones. "You must be one of Charlie's friends."

How could this be Charlie's sister? thought Grace and then, disloyal, *How could you not end up being Charlie if this was your sister?*

"A bit," said Grace, gruffly. She shouldn't feel as if she'd betrayed him—she'd only just met his sister, yes, but she'd known Charlie barely a day.

Cora laughed. "That's always the sum of it. He should have told me. I warned him I'd drop by. This"—she indicated the house generally—"is a lot to deal with. Especially if someone isn't used to real responsibility. He doesn't understand what we have." Then she smiled at Grace, knowingly. "If you're here, perhaps he's finally feeling at home."

Grace did not know what answer was expected, but Cora covered the awkwardness easily. "Of course, it's good for him to be busy. It will keep him out of trouble. And I'm glad he has company. Friends." Cora's sincerity, her frank regard, were warm as remembered sun. Generously, she took no notice of Grace's borrowed clothes.

"He's been kind," said Grace. It was the wrong word.

"Oh, he's not vicious," said Cora. "I wish he was a *little* more assertive. A whole house and I assume he's still keeping himself to the sleep-out."

The daybed, the duffel bag under it; a fragmentary instinct told Grace she should disapprove. But since she had slept on the sofa, she was equally subject to Cora's benevolent pity. It made Grace long to be ordinary, whatever that meant.

"Tea?" said Cora.

As the kettle boiled, Cora sorted through tins of tea at the back of a cupboard, wiped down the counter and set several paint jars, along with the sprouting seed on the windowsill, quietly into the bin. She stacked newspaper strips on the scrapbooks which Charlie must have brought in, and put her handbag on top. Deliberate, confident movements—Cora belonged to a world of certainties. "Please, sit," she said.

Grace obeyed. With Cora right there, she could not believe that anybody ever turned into vines, that urgent secrets hid in this breeze-ridden house, or that anything important could be forgotten. If it were, Cora would turn it out into the daylight.

"Speaking of Charlie," said Cora, smiling, "where is he?"

Grace had no reason not to tell the truth, except the normality of Cora's attention—here in the bright kitchen with teacups between them, steaming with something bitterer and more floral than the tea Charlie made—proved

Grace existed. To say Charlie was searching for a witch at a drowned house would poison that sweetness. Grace dredged up Charlie's lie. "He said he had to go to the shops."

Cora's fingernails rang a single nervous run of notes on the side of her cup. *She's worried*, Grace realised, and asked, "What *type* of trouble did you want him kept out of?"

Cora's smile looked painted on. At last she said, gently, "You ought to be told. Over the years, several people Charlie has known—not *well*, but well enough—have gone missing. These coincidences happen when you don't live the most stable life, but to detectives it looks convenient." She hesitated with a spoon over the sugar jar, then put it down.

"Murder?" asked Grace.

"There's no proof," said Cora. "Just a pattern. There was Lydia Damson, who took off when we were kids. Jess Poll was a distant cousin, and took pity on Charlie when he moved out—Jess headed off on a road trip and probably found a better life. Then Charlie was at uni with Micah, who washed up in the river. Very sad, but—" She gave a little sigh. "Drinking. After that, I got Charlie a job with Stef at a café—there was barely anything between them; Charlie doesn't have the focus for romance." She pulled an apologetic face. "Stef went missing, but there were, ah, underlying issues. And now Alli Kenton, who *tried*. We're worried about Alli—it's been weeks. Charlie hasn't mentioned any of this?"

Pinprick memories flashed with each name—a smell of antiseptic, a window-glass colour. They tangled with Charlie's questions, urgent and alarmed, when he'd first tried to work out who she was.

"He isn't under real suspicion," continued Cora. "He just

doesn't do himself favours by being so *Charlie*. He needs friends to be careful for him."

She glanced at her wrist, and was cheerfully business-like again. "My ride should be here. *Meetings.* They proposed putting a bus depot on the floodplain, of all things! Impractical, yes, but it's green space, and they won't ruin Bellworth's character while a Wren cares."

Grace believed her—the woman's clear confidence must be endlessly persuasive. Cora gathered her bag, her jacket, the sleekness of fresh air and purpose. "Tell Charlie I left rubbish bags under the sink. And call me if he gets too morbid. We'll do drinks." She kissed near Grace's cheek, in a cloud of vanilla perfume. "You didn't have your tea."

She was gone, carrying away the honey-gold light and urgent happiness. The twilight of the house stilled behind her, and Grace realised Cora hadn't drunk her tea, either.

⁂

Charlie, striding along the dream-space of the creek, did not notice the day sliding away. He searched for some feeling deeper than mild regret. Keeping clear of responsibilities, evading the weight of blame and grief and ambition, had got him no further than where he'd started.

His last truly strong emotion had been his dying panic, fourteen years ago. The relapse the day before was only an aftershock. But as other people (not enough) survived worse with their humanity intact, he assumed his lack was due to being a Wren.

Although the path stretched, Charlie was startled out of his thoughts only once. A taste of blood and bile, the tinny shock of a small, unavailing fear, not his. And this time, unlike nights when he woke to check his feet for mud, his hands for scratches, he knew it had not been caused by him, either.

Under the breathless trees, among insects pooling and darting, he waited for a greater epiphany. None came.

Still, mild regret wasn't nothing. He could act on it.

Volney Street, when he reached it, was blue-starred with plumbago, drenched in the honey-butter fragrance of flowering gum. The horizon above the graveyard burned peach and apricot. A flight of ibises, cruciform, sailed in reflection across the window of the taxi driver's house. When he looked up, the sky was empty. He didn't see a girl watching dark-eyed behind the glass.

On the top step at number 21 was a bag of lemons—an unexplained demand, an insistent expectation.

"Grace?" he called as he went in.

Light gleaming through the fretwork above the kitchen door scattered a crawling lace of shadows into the hall. Knots and faces.

Charlie, about to rummage for food, realised the counter had been rearranged. The table was tidy, except for two cups of tea, grown cold. By the door, dirt and a tiny grey feather had been tracked in. The sink looked freshly scrubbed— there was a faint scent of drain cleaner and Ida in the air. And the avocado plant had gone.

He found it in the rubbish bin, fallen into the creased cardboard of a flattened box. A little hurt, he bent to fish it out. He'd be leaving it behind, but that was no excuse for destroying it.

Grace, soundless in the other doorway, watched Charlie slouch around the kitchen, and envied him. He didn't fill out his life, the way Cora did hers. But if something happened to him, his sister, at least, would care. No one had looked for Grace.

Suddenly ferocious, Grace thought, *How* dare *he exist so casually when it's all I want? When I'd tear out a heart and eat it, if that would save me?*

The idea was bloodied by her actions the day before, when she had eaten the—the thing. Dismayed, she felt hunger, and a gnawing memory: a scrap of story of witches and hearts. It belonged to a world without Cora's sunny rationality, without electric kettles and Charlie rummaging in bins. But if hunger drove her to the Wrens' door, if there were witches, and women grown through with vines, why shouldn't eating a human heart fix her?

If Grace was the danger Cora suspected followed her brother, Charlie was right to mistrust her.

He retrieved the avocado seed, shook tea off, pinched its new leaves into shape and returned it to its jar. And Grace thought wildly, *I want that, too. I want time to care about something insignificant.*

Charlie pushed open the screen door at the top of the steps, shoved his hands in his pockets, looked down at the darkening garden.

Hush, Grace said to the hunger. Aloud, she asked, "What did you find out?"

Charlie jumped, and caught himself with one hand on the doorframe. "Making me fall down the stairs?" he said, with forced lightness. "I hear it's not a reliable method."

"I'll remember," said Grace. "Was there a witch?"

When he laughed, the resemblance to Cora faded. Lines

fanned around the corners of his eyes, and he became less *Wren* and more *Charlie*.

"Just an old friend," he said. "Liddy. She didn't want anything to do with me. Fair, I suppose. But she's alive."

After Cora's litany, it was remarkable. "Did she know anything? About me?"

He shook his head. "Just rumours. Whether any of it was useful . . . She wasn't *surprised*, Grace. That's something, isn't it?"

"For you," said Grace. She wished herself in Cora's world, welcoming of Grace but not her strangeness.

Charlie's smile faded. "There was no reason to throw out the avocado."

The breezy normality of Cora's visit would be sullied by dragging it into this moment, so Grace agreed. "It wasn't hurting anyone."

Charlie grimaced. "I guess I understand bad associations." And Grace, prepared to be annoyed at being forgiven for something she hadn't done, was glad when he added, "How are the stitches holding?"

She unbuttoned the outer of her many layers, and let the shirt drop to show him. She already knew why he fell silent. Although the threads held, roses were breaking from her skin. She'd picked their edges loose and seen, in the grey interior of her shoulder, green shoots.

As Charlie adjusted the strings, he said, "It does mean something to me, that Liddy believes this. I had a bad time here—we moved here and our mum died, and Ida didn't want us, and then I was nearly drowned . . . And ever since, I've known things. About the river." Charlie's long hands were carefully impersonal among the vines as he went on. "All of this, you, it's something from the lies we made up as kids. But if Liddy's heard others tell the same stories, and *you're* true, maybe other things are as well."

"What—" began Grace. Then barbed wire wrenched through her stomach, her chest, her neck.

It felt as if her soul was ripped through her spine. Fear surged: survival, snarling hunger. Like a cat on a line, Grace spun, teeth and claws.

Charlie, arms across his face, jumped clear. Grace scrambled around the table.

"I'm sorry, I'm sorry!" Charlie was saying. There was blood on his hands.

Grace's vision was blurred, her throat cinched closed.

"Liddy said—I thought—you didn't hurt before—"

Leaves and bark blocked Grace's lungs; panic thick and dry filled her chest.

"Breathe, Grace!"

Holding out a palm to stop him, she shut her eyes. She made herself draw in air, wheezing, until space stretched between her bending ribs. When she opened her eyes, Charlie was gingerly folding her fingers around a cup of water.

"What did you do?" Her voice was gravel.

"I didn't mean to hurt you!" he said. "I promised I wouldn't! But if the plants were shallow, they'd maybe pull out like a splinter, or if I broke off a piece, we could find out what type of vine . . ."

She stood upright, put down the cup, pressed her sides. She was less strangled, but still furious. "Did you?"

He held up his empty hand, and she saw with malicious satisfaction that it was lacerated, as if he'd dragged thorns through his closed fist.

"I hope it gets *infected*," she rasped. "I hope *you* grow roses, Charlie Wren. Then you'll be sorry."

OPALWOOD

My brother (says Mr Braithe) brought fossilised wood back from one of his trips out west—lumps of petrified trunks and branches from forests old when dinosaurs were young. Beautiful stuff, veined and beaded with opal.

As always, he overdid the thing. He spent his time off prospecting, then started detouring on jobs just to fetch home more examples. The car would pull into the street weighed low with cardboard boxes and fraying sacks.

He lined his collection up across the verandah, stacked it in cabinets, displayed chunks and discs around the picture rail in the living room. Rough stones, and slices polished to mirrors; knobbly rocks still shedding dirt, and jewelled shards winking like eyes.

He lost his job of course, lost his friends, lost interest in anything else. Towards the end—before the last trip, the one he didn't return from—he'd sit in his armchair late into the night with everything turned off, even the fan. But in spite of the silence, he swore to me he could hear long-dead winds moving through those ancient trees.

CHAPTER TEN

An Arrival

Charlie heated beans, then leaned against the stove and ate out of the saucepan—Grace refused food. As he repeated Liddy's stories, he tried not to be disconcerted by Grace's gaze. She didn't blink often, but he supposed he deserved surveillance.

She was restless, though, moving from the kitchen table to the counter and back to the chair, folded with her chin on her knees, stretching suppleness into her arms. Once she gave a pathetic cough—he suspected she meant him to feel bad. From time to time she shook out sugar from its jar and picked at it. He thought of birds picking out the hearts of flowers.

"You're probably feeding the plants," he said. Grace held eye contact and reached for a teaspoon.

"Fine," said Charlie. "You'll have no teeth and a healthy growth of vines. You'll be a—a shrub with gums."

"Hush," said Grace. Roses had crept around the corner of her jaw, the skin at her hairline was dimpled with thorns, but she looked better. Relatively. And she'd accepted the possibility of Liddy's improbable explanations as easily as he had, and taken the idea of a tide of ghosts in stride. In one day he'd found two people who believed the odder parts of his reality, and plunged deeper into it. True, Liddy was angry with him and Grace had a grudge against Wrens; otherwise it was pleasant.

"If your Liddy is right, I will be, anyway," Grace added. "The roses are too far through me. They're tickling at the back of my mind, rustling around my thoughts like branches around birds. I wish the roses did have a will—I could fight that. They don't *want*. They're just . . . growing."

"Like plants," said Charlie, deliberately not glancing at the jar on the windowsill.

"No," said Grace, frustrated. "Someone's idea of a plant, or a drawing come to life. They exist, but they aren't real."

"But you're real," said Charlie. "Think of Liddy's other explanations—you're not a memory."

"The opposite, if anything," murmured Grace, pushing sugar into a pile.

"You have a reflection. And you've changed." A few more days and she'd have made more of her life than he had in fourteen years. "You don't reset. You've chosen a name and found things out."

"I have," she said, then snapped, "I'm a person." She knew human concepts—*camphor* and *wax* and *Wren*.

Charlie, startled, said, "Obviously."

She nodded. "Then of your Liddy's suggestions, we're left with a *nest*. So either I slithered into a tangle of plants and grew through them, which I don't think is a thing people do, or something made a nest of me."

"You'd have to be hollow," said Charlie. "But you're a person, and flowers don't haunt people, do they? Anyway, they're too sharp to be ghosts. So are you."

"If I was somebody left for dead in the water," she began, distantly, "like—was it Micah?"

Charlie, puzzling through the mystery for Grace, felt a chill for his own sake.

"I didn't tell you how they found Micah," he said.

"No." She held his gaze, and then relented. "You asked if I knew the name. But your sister was here today; she told me. About Micah and Alli and—and the others who disappeared."

Charlie wanted to ignore that litany of the missing, the implicit suspicion that fell on him, the risk it was to know him. He could just demand why she hadn't mentioned Cora before. Instead he forced himself to say, "Do you mind?"

"Do you?"

He was generally believed not to. He had acted concerned as required, but he was after all a Wren, and neither housemates nor detectives had ever seemed entirely convinced. Even Alli, before becoming someone else not to care about, once said to his face, on a sigh of cigarette smoke, that it turned out still waters didn't always flow deep. Alli (who'd always carried a reminder not to settle down) had a knack of showing him who he'd need to have been, to escape.

Charlie examined the saucepan and said, for the first time, honestly, "Yes." Then hastily, "What else did Cora say?"

Grace's paper-bark skin, Liddy's superstitions, his fears, this prickly domesticity—Charlie was getting too comfortable among shifting impossibilities. He resented the sudden intrusion into it of his sister—successful, pragmatic, positive.

"That she was going to a meeting about buses, and brought rubbish bags for you. She tidied up." Grace's chin jutted, as if she didn't want to speak about Cora, either. Charlie brightened. People usually liked talking about his sister; he heard their comparative estimation of him slip when they did.

He surprised himself by asking, "Did she find anything to criticise outside?" He pointed to the footprint by the kitchen door. "Or was that you?"

"I haven't been out since yesterday," said Grace. "I—"

There was a thump in the garden.

⚜

Charlie took a torch, but the air was still peach-lit. From the top of the steps, where the weathered handrail bent down, the yard looked empty.

"Probably the kid," he said. He was overdue a visit from the girl's father, furious and suspicious. But the police hadn't checked in yet, either.

"There was something in the garden yesterday," said Grace, at his shoulder.

"You didn't say anything."

She ignored him. "It was a shambling mess of sticks and cords, but I—I ran."

Charlie, so recently attacked by her, said, "That's not like you."

Grace folded her arms stiffly. "Something else attacked it. And that I *couldn't* see."

"Well, there's two of us now," said Charlie.

They descended into twilight. Cool dampness rose around them, the spice of daylit leaves overwhelmed by the perfume of white flowers. Standing in the grass, the dusty under-house yawning dry at their backs, they looked up at a green sky, flecked by one or two stars and a few grey moths.

There was no sign of Grace's visitor.

The yard withdrew into gloom. Charlie imagined it as a path, leading through evenings in other gardens, wastelands behind streets, labyrinths of fishbone ferns and spider lilies.

"You could bury me out here," said Grace, practically.

Charlie was thinking of a reply when something rustled. He swung the torch's beam under the house.

"The shed," said Grace.

But all inside was as it should be. The art project on a bench along the far wall, the old grass-cutter, the shrouding tarps. Something scurried under a crate.

"There," said Grace. She wrenched the shovel out of its stand.

"A lizard," said Charlie.

When the shed door closed and the footsteps moved away, the taxi driver's daughter unfolded herself from behind a workbench.

That afternoon, she had sweated her way to the library and borrowed the few local histories she could find: *Unsolved Crimes and Mysteries of Western Gowburgh* and *River City Tombstones: Gowburgh's Spectral Celebrities*, which were by a professor. They'd had many footnotes, few thrills, and nothing about the Wren house; when Mr Wren passed in the street, she'd abandoned the struggle. She was allowed to go into the yard at number 21 and—since Cora must have left—she wouldn't be embarrassed.

But the shed was darker than she'd expected, and some of the professor's stories lingered. She was not comforted by sounds that only *might* be lizards, and almost certainly weren't a ghost dog, and whatever his sister said, she didn't want Mr Wren to find her.

Through the dirty wired windowpane, she watched him and the torch and the swamp-woman. Cora Wren wouldn't wear old jeans or long shirts buttoned to wrist and neck, as if it was winter. Cora Wren would certainly not be frightened by lizards.

The girl felt friendlier towards the creek-woman.

⚬

In the marine light, Grace didn't respond to Charlie's glance, or explain her fear. The urge to jump at a lizard and eat it wasn't human; Charlie didn't need to know.

Behind them, the clothesline twisted, squeaking like violins.

The trees—fruiting and flowered—were weightless as seaweed, buoyed by the cooling air. Grace imagined pushing off and gliding, feet trailing through ferns.

A bat unfurled from a branch with a leathery snap.

She shouldn't have let Charlie convince her to come outside. The thickening layers of her muscles slowed her. She was trammelled by rose stems and the consciousness that people disappeared around Charlie Wren. He'd told her he planned to leave Gowburgh—perfect timing for one last disappearance.

Of course, if he'd meant to kill her, he could have torn the vines out entirely. Used a knife. Wrapped her in the shower curtain and dragged her down the stairs. . . . Perhaps it was easier to let her walk.

Grace shook her head. Her mind still felt jagged, held together by string. Charlie, she reminded herself, had been kinder than necessary to a stranger who forced her way into his house.

If, of course, he *was* a stranger.

She touched the back of her head. There were divots where her skull should have curved smoothly; the yielding roughness of felted matter. The rustling intrusions were not imaginary—her thoughts weren't her own.

Charlie was ahead of her, loose-limbed, alert. But this was his house. Wren land. He knew its cavernous under-growth . . .

Grace stopped. "I'll wait here," she said.

<hr>

In the shed, the rummaging noises grew bolder, and the air beside the girl felt calmly alert. But when she waved her hand, she touched nothing.

She peered through the dirty glass. If her dad found her gone after dark, he'd call the police. And if he discovered she'd been *trespassing* . . .

The woman, drawn-in on herself, had stopped where the yard dissolved into night. She would be easy to outrun. The girl stood on tiptoe to see where Mr Wren had gone.

<hr>

Charlie carried the shovel—Grace had relinquished it quickly. *Fingerprints,* said paranoia. *False innocence.*

But Grace looked as if she expected to be dragged on-ward, so he said, "Keep an eye on the house?"

She nodded tightly.

The yard was immense—someone could be lurking in it. Yet, reluctant as he was to feel at home indoors, it was impossible not to in the garden. The rustling night was companionable, the earth familiar. His awareness lifted into the branches, growing with them, pushing up into new leaves, budding fruit through the boughs. The graves he knew were here—Dennis, the pigeon, no doubt other animals (a cat, he guessed, indistinctly)—were small and quiet.

He played the torch down the slope. The shadow-lace of leaves gathered over the uneven ground, deepening it into pits. A streamer of mist drifted ragged from the crease along the rear fence, still damp where the last rain had drained between the yards.

It was too quiet. No barking a street over. No traffic.

He turned back. Far away Grace, framed by black leaves, faced the house. The kitchen light outlined her hair and shoulders, but the shape of her was wrong.

Standing behind her, close enough to touch, was another person.

⚜

Grace, watching the lit grass, was glad Charlie was out of reach with the shovel. It had abraded her hands; her arms had bowed under its weight. Its iron, rising in rust, reminded her of decay.

Indoors, the threat was herself—thorns raking inside her shoulders, the vegetable pressure of flowers under her tongue, peeling skin that softened when washed, but kept separating. She shifted from foot to foot, in case the garden's *aliveness* called roots down through the soles of her borrowed shoes.

Charlie's acceptance of what ought to horrify him was no use to Grace. But Cora, sunlit, would laugh the worst away, and shake her head over Charlie. Then she and Cora would leave, out among city lights, glittering people, dusted with life like birds in pollen.

And for a moment, in place of the house, Grace *saw* it, the distant centre of Gowburgh—flickering buildings, misaligned. Among them, fractured selves she had been overlapped and reached to Cora. The images guttered, offset and inconsistent, but her own.

She was grateful enough that it made her feel kindlier towards Charlie. He hadn't given her this memory; she could trust him more freely if she had something to trust him with.

Heavy-footed, he tramped through the grass, and dropped his hand on her shoulder—but Charlie's hand had been there before she had a name.

"Nothing, then?" she said, leaning slightly back.

"No—thing," came the answer, rasped and stilted. Then the hand contorted around her neck, dragging against rose-thorns, tightening as the fingers of another slid sharp and ruthless into her hair, and tore at her skull.

⚜

The taxi driver's daughter noticed the thing when the creek-woman did—a bad sketch of a human, stiff-limbed and hollow, stretching too-thin arms. A gust of air left the shed, as if racing to see.

The woman *changed*. She didn't freeze, or scream. She spun slashing, clawing at the thing's face—or where a face should have been.

Then Mr Wren brought the shovel down.

⚜

Grace had fallen with her attacker. She dragged herself from beneath what remained—it was weightless as a paper wasp's nest—and watched Charlie lower the shovel.

He'd dropped the torch. In the yellow glow from the house, his face looked sickly.

"I could have—" he began. "I killed—"

"*Look* at it," snapped Grace. Charlie didn't deserve to be in shock. He hadn't been mauled. And only that morning he had mended her—this was hardly his first encounter with a creature of sticks and leaves.

The mannequin lay shattered and splayed, rotten plant-matter clotted with webs and soil. Its face, if it ever had one, had crumbled.

"It's like Liddy's nests," said Charlie. "She said they weren't made to walk."

The shovel had sliced the thing from almost-shoulder to almost-hip, leaving no blood, no splintered bone. How had she mistaken it for a person? She touched her own throat. It didn't look as if it could have had a voice.

Knots of vine and string sprang apart as she watched, bark unrolled—not as if savaged, but simply as if life no longer held it together. Dead leaves and wingless beetles fell out. A strip of rotting fabric untwisted from around a sun-bleached snail shell. The grass ruffled as if with escaping air—Grace scrambled out of its path.

Barely anything remained.

⁕

In the shed, a draught whispered among tarpaulins and bags. The art project glinted, empty as a bowl. The girl decided to abandon it, and make something else—she didn't want that face sitting pale in her room.

Outside, Mr Wren picked up a piece of what she hoped was ribbon and put it in his pocket. Then he walked towards the shed.

She ducked. There was a wooden knock on the wall, and the door shivered, but he didn't come in.

When she looked out again, Mr Wren and the creek-woman had climbed the stairs. The spill of brightness from the kitchen was shut off. The windows closed, mottling the silhouettes inside. Light retreated deeper into the house.

The taxi driver's daughter exhaled, and pushed the shed door.

It was latched.

BAD MICE

I was born out west (says Edith's cousin Mavis). One year, there was a mouse plague. They destroyed crops and carried disease. Sometimes they glimmered out of the grass in a velvet sheet, and carried cars off the road, like swift water. Mostly, I remember the smell.

My father, not kind, concocted traps and poisons—cruel poisons, clever traps. They didn't work. When the tides of mice receded elsewhere, ours lingered. They slid down piano strings, gnawed through saddles, winked in the pantry, and ate, and ate, and ate.

My father finally let the neighbours give me a cat. An excellent mouser, they said. But it ignored the mice. It tucked its paws under itself, and looked away.

When the neighbours drove over with old dresses for me, my father shut the cat in the bathroom with a dozen mice; it leapt onto the windowsill, staring towards its old home.

"See?" said my father. "Useless! No killer instinct."

"What were you expecting?" the neighbours asked. "You put it in an empty room."

My father showed them grain bins glossy with bodies, droppings thick as sorghum. The neighbours claimed they saw nothing—there were no mice, and the plague was over.

But not for my father.

Shortly after that, I was taken away to school in Gowburgh. I never went home.

CHAPTER ELEVEN

Suspicions

The taxi driver's daughter shook the shed door.

The latch held. The kitchen windows stayed unlit. She tried to be glad no one had heard her, but when she blinked, she saw the afterimage of the shovel descending, the corpse falling into leaves.

She could still call for help. But first, she fumbled for a light switch among coldly clanking tools. At least the sound covered the breeze that hissed through the shed, the shuffling of small bodies among boxes. The slithering of dust.

⚬

Grace watched Charlie's shoulder jitter, and waited for him to speak. But he boiled the kettle, filled two mugs, and carried them to the parlour without saying a word. Grace followed with the sugar, closing doors on looming silence.

When she was on the sofa, and Charlie on the floor with his knees bent high as a grasshopper's, he opened his mouth, shut it, then said, "Did it hurt you?"

Grace touched her hair. Her scalp was crumbling. She felt rummaged-in, her thoughts chipped. She pushed her crushed throat into shape and rasped, "I'm fine." Her neck was scraped, sticky more with sap than blood.

"I'm used to strange things," said Charlie, abruptly. "I can sense the river system, even from here."

Grace wasn't sure of his point. "Useful?" she managed.

He shrugged. "If it were possible to be lost in Gowburgh, maybe." He turned the mug of tea between his hands. "If I focus, I can sense what's in the water. No fun in floods, but rarely good. So much decay. The one time I nerved myself up to practice—to close my eyes and reach out into that feeling—I found a body. It took some explaining to convince anyone it was an accident."

Charlie was talking for himself. Grace drew a cautious breath, testing the bellows-wheeze of her lungs, and was startled when he turned to face her, his elbow on the sofa by her feet.

"I stopped looking in," he said. "There were people I didn't want to find rotted . . . But I know strange, and I haven't seen anything like *that*."

Grace, fingers on the cracking wicker of her ribs, did not point out the obvious. "Should I say it was a trick of the light?"

Roses had pushed through her cheek into her mouth. They tasted cotton-dry.

"No!" Charlie, still pale, grinned. "I'm glad you saw it. It's proof I didn't imagine it."

Her sense of humour had escaped along a new fracture. Mentally, she pulled herself together—there was *less*. Physically, she picked at roughened skin around her nails, splintered in the fight.

"Did you recognise it?" he asked eagerly.

If she had, the knowledge—carefully cultivated—was gone. Twig-fingers had clawed it out of her skull.

"Why did it attack you?"

"I wasn't armed," she said drily.

He'd swung the shovel so easily. He hadn't enjoyed it—she'd seen his face immediately after—but now he was evading guilt. Grace refused to pretend the attack was interesting; not if Charlie might strike as certainly when confronted with another shambling gnarl of plant life.

Her coiled ferocity was exhausted; a mass pushed against the back of one eye. A headache, she lied to herself, if she felt pain. And she was afraid to explain to Charlie her certainty the creature had not sought to destroy her.

It had been trying to get in.

⚜

There was no switch. The taxi driver's daughter groped for a file or chisel and lost her way. The window's charcoal rectangle was too small in the shed's darkness. Reaching out, she touched a papery carapace—her art project.

Reoriented, she kept searching, dirt and oil caking her hands. And again, she was at the back of the building.

The third time, she felt herself pulled as if by strong shallow water. Sweat and shivers wrapped her legs like wet hair, caught against scabs on her shins, then lingeringly dragged free.

She breathed slowly, to keep from panicking. The darkness smelled less of shed, and more of damp earth, cigarette smoke, sugary medicine, and the soft stink of condolence flowers rotting in a vase.

Charlie's mind, adrenaline-fuelled, darted and shied from too many things. The figures in the trees. Liddy's anger. Vengeful spirits. A shovel slicing through neck and torso.

Worst, he was grateful.

Dreaming so often of deaths, he'd feared the dreams were true—that was the other reason he'd stopped searching the water. Now he could compare the dreams to this.

Yet he'd also felt, in that moment, more real—and a fragile, terrifying wonder had been torn apart.

He shook away an image, unwanted, of the shovel cutting instead into Grace's shoulder, and drank tea to scald out the nausea. This was shock. Innocent of dream-murders, he had, awake, done something irrevocable. It hadn't been a person, but it had looked like one. It had moved with intent. It had, perhaps, been innocent.

Perhaps.

Out of his pocket, he took the torn cloth he'd collected. A fraying strip of spotted fabric, filthy. He sniffed it—damp earth. A tassel, matted and burred, clung to a corner.

He held it out. "It was in the"—not corpse, not *body*—"remnants. Ring any bells?"

Grace put down the sugar jar, turned the scrap over, and frowned.

"A flicker," she said.

He hadn't expected recognition; certainly not confession. But Grace, one hand pushed through her hair, said, relieved, "It's a new memory. One *I* made." Intrigue brightened her eyes. "One of the missing people."

"Alli Kenton," he said. Wearing that knotted summer scarf, amusedly pretentious in all photographs, all seasons.

Wearing it the day Alli stopped seeing Charlie, which was shortly—too short for comfort—before anyone stopped seeing Alli.

Charlie hadn't looked for a body. He'd learned that lesson. It would have made others ask why he'd known where to look, and ended the ache of hope that Alli—glamorous with sunglasses and a light bag, and without him—had boarded a plane for somewhere cosmopolitan. It would have undermined Cora's careful coaching that he and Alli were barely friends.

It wasn't entirely untrue; their breakup had been more an acknowledgement that Alli struggled to notice Charlie even when he was in the room. It had been a relief not constantly trying to be interesting.

But soon after, he'd had the old dream, except it was Alli's face sinking into darkness like the moon, clouded by tasselled cloth. This fabric smelled the same as the water in his dream. It raised Alli from those flat memories—vital and fascinating and scornful.

"It's a scarf," said Grace, wonderingly. "I saw it in a photo—a flyer in one of the scrapbooks."

So Aunt Ida had thought about him. Or at least, kept up with the news.

Grace, wincing, peeled the cloth off her fingertips and handed it back.

"Coincidence?" said Charlie. He didn't want that thing to have done something to Alli. To have been, however slightly, Alli . . .

Grace stared. "A cousin of yours disappears, and this is a coincidence?"

"Alli wasn't a cousin. That's Jess." Cora had been informative.

"Some relation, anyway," said Grace. "There were family trees in those boxes, and I saw a Kenton on them. I noticed because you'd said the name. I remembered, because I don't have much else to remember."

She spoke impatiently, like Liddy—as if he squandered family to spite her.

"We went *out*," said Charlie in disgust.

Grace looked unsurprised. For all Charlie knew, the document had suggested it was common. The city sprawled, but was not large, and the Wrens, for better or worse, had lived here since free settlement. Possibly a few years before that. The city probably crawled with third cousins five times removed. They weren't a close family. What were the chances Stef or Micah had been distantly related, too?

He unfolded from the floor and marched back to the dim kitchen. There, the night was audible around the house, small noises and soft mysterious collisions. The avocado leaves swayed in front of their distorted reflection. He returned with the box of papers and his phone.

He'd missed a message from Cora, checking in. All this was her fault—she'd introduced them, although later she'd disapproved of Alli's attempts to change him. He emptied the box onto the floor and sorted through, but found no family tree and fewer scrapbooks.

Grace claimed ignorance. "I didn't want them," she said. "It was newspaper articles and"—she closed her eyes— "obituaries and eisteddfods. Memorials." Bitter and tired, she added, "Wrens being Wrens."

Wrens in the Bellworth Business Chamber. Wrens behind cake stalls and raffling prizes; Wrens with corsages and gloves: Bellworth Belles and Beaus. On war memorials and property deeds, park signs and graveyards. Wrens the whole way down to however they'd dug their first foothold.

Nothing for Grace to steal. If she had, he'd have known. He'd seen how readily thoughts and alarm darted across Grace's face when she was unguarded; the rest of the time she was all spikes or studiously blank. Now she was eating sugar on the sofa, weariness wilting the roses.

Yet everything she wore was taken from his house. Even her name. What did it say about Charlie that he'd accepted her this quickly as a friend?

His sister would point out—

"Cora," he realised. "She must have taken them." He reached for his phone to send a belated reply. Cora never answered calls. "She got into family history. Liddy used to laugh at her."

Grace changed position so stiffly it ought to have hurt. Charlie winced, but Grace was thinking.

"That thing," she said. "Which of your Liddy's categories was it? Unless—could she have built it?"

Liddy, crouching on the suburb's fringe, sculpting scarecrows from rubbish . . . If she'd had the power to make something as marvellous as that monster, why waste time being annoyed with him? Why send it to attack Grace? They hadn't met, as far as he knew.

Grace eased down to lie along the sofa. "This can't be the only place odd things appear," she said. "Don't you talk to your neighbours?"

"I don't live here," he reminded them both, conscious of how few people he knew well enough to ask anything useful. A message from Cora distracted him. First "Yes" and then "Come out! Get a life! Qs re your 'friend.'"

"You didn't go to them, either," he said to Grace. Even

Aunt Ida had been more patronising than neighbourly. And Cora wouldn't thank him for involving outsiders in what was increasingly a family matter.

People notice, Liddy had said. Not *People know.* But what if everyone in Gowburgh had monsters in their gardens, or—better—ways to keep them out? If mysteries like the creature, and whatever was happening to Grace, were real, someone somewhere must be curious.

A flash of impatience on Grace's face. "At least asking would be doing something!"

"And say what?" Charlie countered. "I killed someone in the backyard? We ripped a clue in a missing person case out of the chest of a plant-person? You didn't want the police called, either."

Grace levered herself onto her elbow. She looked pinched, her hairline mottled by roses. "I'm falling apart," she said. "Charlie . . ." Fear, doubt, anger crossed her face. "What if that thing is what I will *become*?"

Charlie didn't have a reply. Grace lowered herself again, but when she spoke, she was determined. "I need an answer. Tomorrow. Whatever happens."

He glanced at the door's unlit panes. The shops would be closed; throughout the neighbourhood tow trucks and delivery vans would be parked on footpaths and in front yards. Sleep called.

But it was not so late. Certainly not for Cora. And however ordered her reality, she knew all sorts of people. Tonight—she'd texted details—she was at a book launch for a local historian. If he wanted information on oddities, he might not have to ask Cora.

He stood. "I'm going out for a bit."

Grace wouldn't crumble this evening. In the garden,

she had fought. In the kitchen, she'd nearly got her hands around *his* neck.

Despite the swinging lamp, her eyes were mud dark. A gaze out of someone's nightmare. He knew he should be alarmed by Grace, not for her. What if he woke from drowning dreams to find her bent blank-faced over him, stained green by streetlights, a clawed hand outstretched—

She hadn't killed him yet.

He stooped and tapped her shoulder awkwardly. The roses smelled soft as old soap.

"Sleep," he said. "You'll be safe inside. I'll see what I can find out."

But he remembered, uncomfortably, the pigeon in the ceiling—something had got it. He closed the door carefully behind him.

In the shed, the current of air washed the girl's feet out from under her. She crashed down between paint cans and grass cutters, grazed her elbow on metal, slammed her chin against a wooden corner. But there was no time to cry: the draught by the floor was *inquisitive*. She clamped her injured arm against her side, and pulled her t-shirt over her mouth and nose.

"Help!" she yelled. Her throat was dry. "*Help.*" Now that she needed an adult, sound was slow as cold honey. Breath squeaked between her teeth, like—like a whistle.

She had an idea.

"Here-here-here," she shout-whispered. "Come here! I'll give you real food, not sticks and crusts." She patted her knee, encouraging, frantic. "You can sleep on my bed. Please *be* here!"

Then the weightlessness of something once-dense pressed against her ribs, and—faint as forgetting—the wonderful stink of animal. The crowded breeze turned its many attentions away from her and flowed on.

"*Good* boy," gasped the girl. "*Good* dog. Let's get out."

The girl and the presence scrambled in utter darkness towards the pencil-grey window. She hauled herself up the workbench, onto her feet.

Behind, pressure gathered. Paper knocked against boxes and tarps, rustling closer. She refused to turn. Raking through tools, she found a piece of metal, thin and sharp-edged, and with a hiss of pain, worked it off its nail and faced the door.

Her shoulder blades twitched—at any moment she expected hands to paw at her back. The blade bit, shaking, between the door and its frame and knocked the latch up. Then she flung the door open and herself through.

She slammed it behind her, and on the third try got the latch into place.

Nothing hurled itself against the door. The walls did not rattle. Nothing misted on the glass.

The girl pushed herself away from the shed and staggered into the blue-green night, gulping ordinary air like water. Alone, except for a pale glint in the trampled grass: a snail shell, coiled and beautiful. She bent, picked it up, and felt briefly as she would have if a wet nose pressed against her face. Shakily, she laughed and straightened.

She wondered, with an unfamiliar sense of responsibility, whether she should warn anyone that something dragging and clawing and *many* was in the shed, and decided Mr Wren could deal with it himself. He had a shovel.

Giddy with triumph, thrilled with terrors and possibilities, she crept alongside the high fence, past wide ferns and rib-leafed palms. When she glanced diagonally up, she could see the underneath of the high-set house, pale threads shining between the floorboards. Timbers creaked, as if someone was walking inside.

She slipped through the jasmine-drenched front yard and over the gate. A possum climbed hand-over-hand along a wire, soft tail whipping for balance. A flying fox, broad-winged, dipped low.

"Let's go home," she said to her companion, and trotted downhill, hoping her father was having a busy night. Coils of gutter-mist sparkled in the lemonade glow of the street-light.

But halfway there, the reassuring presence diminished. When she reached her driveway, it was gone entirely, and she went into the empty house alone.

BURNING BRIGHT

Believe it or not (says young Joe Eising), more than a hundred years ago there used to be a tiger farm near here. Up at the back of Greenstone, where the barracks are now—they wouldn't have stood for it in Bellworth. I've seen photographs: men with handlebar moustaches and women in dark dresses and wide hats leaning on a split-rail fence. If you looked close, you'd see, mottled in black-and-white shadows, a big cat prowling by.

The tigers escaped one too many times, so the government (such as it was then) shut the place down. Sent the surviving animals to faraway zoos.

But I've heard soldiers up there say they've felt a presence stalking them through the eucalypts and the guavas. Even my uncle, when he ran the officers' mess, said he stepped outside once and saw something flow between the wattle trees like a reversal of light and shade, and eyes golden as oranges watching him through the leaves.

CHAPTER TWELVE

A Party

After Charlie changed into his one presentable outfit (long sleeves, *rolled* up—Cora would laugh but Alli had been particular), he wheeled the bicycle up through the graveyard, coasted down the lane to Braithe, and sped along Bellworth Road. The old tyres held, and the brakes mostly worked; Charlie was glad not to be on foot, alone in a night dark as sapphire—as his mother's ring, which had never seemed blue at all. Water-echoes streamed around him, and this time he cut through the parks, rattling over the footbridge.

Then back into streets, through scents of dinners unreformed by decades—peas, lamb, potato. New missing-pet leaflets fluttered on poles. Past the church hall leaking bagpipe music, the rhythm of feet.

The tide of renovation—sprawling supermarkets, charming cafés, repainted fences—had washed around the suburb. The bakery, its sherbet cones and kidney pies shut in for the evening, had changed nothing but its prices. The op-shop glinted with souvenir teaspoons and orphaned port glasses—soon Aunt Ida's anodised cups and mismatched knives would join them. Hand-painted signs on the butcher's windows printed shadows onto stainless trays: *KNOW where your MEAT is FROM.*

When the road turned uphill, the bike frame began creaking ominously. Charlie left it at the station car park as a coal train, brilliant with graffiti, dove through the platform lights, and sank again.

He climbed out of Bellworth proper, above the railway into a region of poplars, sleek cars, and many-balustraded houses. How to explain these unlikely few days to Cora? *So, the backyard is infested with walking trees. . . . Surprise—our inheritance comes with an angry swamp-woman! Oh, and Liddy's living along the creek.* Cora would simply look pained. He imagined Liddy's reaction to that.

Cora probably didn't even remember Liddy.

At his destination, garlands of stark bulbs looped along the high white pickets, and through the gate wound granite paths formal with catering staff. Behind him was night.

The party spilled around lawns, crested on balconies, broke against the tennis court's art deco fence. But his sister was as easy to find as if they were weights sliding on a string. Charlie, evading conversations, glanced up and saw her descending the butterfly stairs. She gleamed in a metallic cocktail dress, her face softened by swinging lanterns and society. She was in her habitat, and exactly as she'd decided to be.

She would fix everything.

"Come upstairs and meet our host," she said, linking her arm through his. On the first landing, she added, "Grace is an odd girl. Have you known her long?"

"No," said Charlie. "She needed a place to stay—"

He already struggled to imagine number 21 without Grace.

"Maybe not *our* house," said Cora, judicially. Problem solved.

On the wide verandah were white-clothed tables and champagne, and a tucked-away display of books, grey-faced as tombstones. No one was looking at them.

"I appreciate you taking care of the house," Cora went on. "I've been frantically busy—but the bus depot is being relocated to Greenstone! I like this colour scheme for number 21. Telephone black and eggshell—"

"I can't wait to sell it," confessed Charlie.

Cora laughed, then turned over his scratched hand. "What happened?" She lowered her voice. "You haven't had any trouble?"

Charlie hesitated. The scratches were real, and so was Grace, and therefore so was the thing which, for want of a better word, he must call a ghost, and his own sense of water and what it carried. He could have pointed to where the river soaked through the night, braided with the thread of Bellworth Creek.

If he told Cora about any of that, or his panic, she would call it a nightmare, a flashback. Charlie didn't want to trade his new certainty, not even for sympathy.

"Gardening," he said. "Anyway, who's the guest of honour?"

"A sudden interest in culture?" teased Cora. "There *is* someone I want to introduce you to." She reached up and smoothed his collar. "Then you can settle down and raise little Wrens."

"Cora!"

She grinned. The world generally went as Cora wanted.

Before she could be distracted by schemes, he pulled her towards the wall, and warned her about Alli's scarf.

Cora glanced over both shoulders before she took the evidence. "In our backyard?" she whispered.

"I know you didn't get on, but did you know Alli was related to us?"

Cora, frowning, turned the scrap over. Charlie couldn't see her face, only the top of her gleaming hair. "Cobweb connection," she murmured. "And it was disappointment, not disapproval. There's no way to prove this is Alli's." He was sure, but before he could invent a plausible explanation, she looked up at him and said, "When did you find out?"

"Grace saw it in a family tree. Did you take the scrapbooks?"

Cora tucked the shred into his pocket. "The library has a Wren archive. They're safer there. Don't look surprised. It's small—we don't keep much and I can only guess what Ida wasted—and makes hardly any sense if you haven't got the trick of it, but we are among the first families."

"English families," said Charlie, out of habit.

Cora waved that away. "Just because some North Gowburgh old-money kids think they were set down by the hand of fate—" She'd attended a good school on a scholarship, and it still rankled. As she glanced down across the garden at her people, dissatisfaction pinched her face. She deserved admiration, but he suspected she didn't always like her court. Charming as she could be, she never kept particular friends long.

She smoothed her expression. "Once you've *got* the place, it's what you do with it that counts. Must you stand so near? I'm going to hurt my neck talking to you."

She accepted two tall glasses from a passing waiter, who

winked at her, then she said, "I don't like your Grace taking an interest. Not with the police still looking for Alli. It's dangerous."

A threat to Cora's career, too: eventually, mud would stick. But it was illogical to refuse his sister's help. She could have washed her hands of him any number of times, and inviting him here proved she'd support him.

Charlie, at risk of being accused of looming, folded his arms and leaned closer. "What if we track down Alli? Or save someone else?"

"Save who? From what?" said Cora. "People leave. You should be used to that. Take the champagne."

Grace, from blue roses. It sounded unbelievable to him here, where the living were in linen and lipstick, where the wide verandah was solid and the fretted brackets freshly painted. Where he was merely Charlie Wren, ex-victim, ex-barista, ex–admin assistant. Current person of interest. Cora's brother.

"Is this about your dreams again?" she asked, kindly. "They're not premonitions. People fall through the cracks in a city, Charlie. Creeks take what they want. It's nobody's fault."

"But if we can prove I had nothing to do with it," he said, "the whole problem will go away."

"Not if you constantly bring it up," Cora snapped. She closed her eyes, folded her hands around the stem of her champagne flute, and was calm. "Charlie. Don't get more involved. Is it Grace? If you think she'll accuse you of something, or that she's *done* something, my friends can make enquiries. It's what police are for. And if she won't leave, they'll remove her. It's our house—"

"I'll talk to her," promised Charlie.

"What if she's dangerous? You're very calm about living with a possible criminal."

"It's a change from wondering if I'm one. This is a great party, by the way, Cora. I'm having a wonderful time."

As he intended, Cora lost patience, and propelled him along the verandah. It was turreted and gazeboed and hung with cascades of trailing succulents. He put his glass on a passing windowsill. The ceiling on the other side had a central plaster moulding larger than a bathtub.

They ran a gauntlet of greetings from young public servants, artier businesspeople, and several creative types he'd met at other events. He heard someone say, as they passed a knot he was sure were poets, "Shit, there's two of them." But Cora's cut-glass smile didn't shatter, and everyone else was delighted—Cora collected admirers, and these approved of Charlie by association, as Alli had. At first.

It was why he'd wanted to be a stranger elsewhere, on his own terms; why he missed Grace's resentment, the girl on the gate's suspicion. But he was here for a reason.

Charlie hadn't heard anyone discussing books, had seen no concentration around a notable guest. But Cora dragged him to where an older man stood self-consciously apart. With cheerful malice, she introduced him as Dr Anderton, *distinguished* author, and glittered away.

Dr Anderton looked as if he would gladly have been addressed as *Professor*, if Gowburgh only permitted it. He was officiously grateful to be delivered an audience. He also referred to Charlie's sister as "our Cora," which grated. "It's about time our Cora ran for council. She'll finish up as lord mayor."

Charlie steered conversation onto the book. Dr Anderton quickly pointed out that his interest was in historically verifiable incidents, evidenced by reliable witnesses, uncontaminated in transmission—no cultural superstitions or substance-induced hallucinations.

Charlie clung to the sensation of aliveness he'd felt earlier, but the immediacy—the horror of the descending shovel, of the thing's decay (not Grace, not Alli)—faded. Reality washed over him. He thought, *I'm drowning again. And for once, I was trying to save someone else.*

He saw Cora across the partygoers, playing her listeners like instruments, glowing just as she had at sixteen, when she first found fame. He raised a hand to her in surrender.

Dr Anderton was explaining, sorrowfully, that his was the academic's unsentimental eye; he operated within an objective tradition, above these modern so-called paranormal investigators or, worse, purveyors of fictions, like a certain histrionic and overwrought exhibition staged in City Hall by a *collective*—

Strings of lights fizzed on a breeze heavy with citronella and aftershave. Beyond the railway, Grace was unravelling. Charlie steeled himself to cut the historian off, and was interrupted by a short board member—he didn't catch which board—in large glasses, who entered the conversation with glasses of wine and a smile suggesting Cora's matchmaking. Saving him again, always.

Guiltily, Charlie sacrificed his rescuer to the professor, scooped a handful of chocolates from a lead-crystal bowl, and escaped.

Downhill, the balmy air thickened. Charlie's certainty (of strangeness, of failure) seeped back. Descending into stagnant memories, he recalled what Liddy said: deaths weren't flowing to wherever they were meant to go. He pictured ghosts slipping down gutters; storm drains slimy with the hair of drowners.

A train left the station, windows yellow as a spirit level. Charlie retrieved the bicycle and wheeled it homeward, wondering how long Liddy thought there'd been a problem. Perhaps his feeling for the river was familiarity with the path he should have taken, and he'd been meant to die years ago.

He'd been fourteen, holding one-handed to a sapling and hanging idly out over the creek, waiting for Liddy. The water level had been dangerously high, although the sky was clear. He'd ignored the usual noises: bush turkeys kicking up causeways of leaves; a pheasant coucal reeling through the branches; kids or old Bill (and he understood now that Bill had not been, perhaps, so old) tramping through the undergrowth.

Something had struck him, he'd heard running feet, and someone shout, "*Wren!*"

Then only confusion, broken water, a final breath before he lost his footing for good.

"*—sink into the mud—just as much trouble—get away—*"

Words, distorted and ferocious. And with his last pure emotion, he had wanted very much *not* to die. *No, no, no—* breath rising shining out of him, irrecoverable—*I never wanted to be in Bellworth, I'll leave forever, if only . . .*

Pain, needles in his lungs, a slash seared across shoulder and chest. He'd been yanked up, spitting and retching.

A hand in his hair, pulling him out or pushing him under. Shouts overhead: Cora's snarl and a man roaring, "You little *bitch*!" And "Give it over!"

Then Charlie *left*.

Through every cut and abrasion, death and mud rushed in. The slope, the channel, the flow to the river, which he carried with him still.

But he was being rescued, although he hadn't known it. Cora, an excellent swimmer, had kicked them away from the old man and hidden them in mud and weeds, holding on to submerged fence-posts until it was safe.

His first memory of after was of sprawling on the bank, lungs and veins sanded raw. Cora's hair streamed around her face, haloed like an icon by sun, and her hand held his although there wasn't any warmth at all. Unsteady, too pale except for where her shirt was pink with her own blood, Cora had said furiously, "You'd better not die now!"

She willed him back to life. He'd stumbled towards the creek before neighbours and ambulance officers carried him away. Cora scolded him then and again, when the cuts were infected, when he was sick from what he'd swallowed. Aunt Ida had no time for malingering nephews; even Liddy thought he was exaggerating, he'd been told. It was Cora who forced Charlie into the sun, onto the grass, into the world.

Her own wound healed quickly, and heroism suited her. She'd gleamed like a medal.

No one was charged. Someone gave Bill an alibi. But Charlie had seen him: face broken by water and rage, grasping an old kitchen knife. Charlie needed to remind himself of that, because sometimes he dreamed he himself held the knife, smooth against his palm. It was as if the confusion of panic and fever had dissolved his memories into someone else's, and put them together wrong.

In those nightmares, the hands fighting off the blade, gripping his wrist, were not his own.

But no one died that day, and maybe no one had to now. Charlie, as he reached home through the sleeping suburb, held that certainty like a cool quartz stone.

The Fifth Day

MORNING

UNDERFLOOR

There are small deaths hidden behind the floors and walls of more houses than you'd think (says the plumber from Braithe Street). Birds to sound an alarm; cats to patrol; dogs to catch what sneaks through. There are still a few builders who, in spite of hi-vis and steel-capped boots and certifications, know how to set a caretaker under a threshold, and a guardian in the foundations.

As for houses which don't come with that built in, you'd be surprised how many families have their own ways of keeping things out—or controlling them. Even if it's only to harness the idea of spirits to get someone to behave. Of course, some will just ignore a shadow, a cupboard, a whole room. Occasionally, ghosts are a thing inconvenient people become.

And not all the bones under houses are small.

CHAPTER THIRTEEN

The Library

The taxi driver's daughter slept badly. Moths billowed against the moonlight; bats quarrelled in the mango tree. Her mother used to say bats were good luck; it wasn't *them* you heard screaming in the branches. The bleached snail shell on the sill whispered under the ceiling fan.

In the morning, barefoot, she added it to the shells bordering the garden. Several had split or cracked. When she was little, she'd asked her mother why they were there, and been told, "Warnings." After her mother died, she'd asked her dad who the warning was for, and he'd said, "Snails." Well, perhaps there were snails and *snails*.

"And *stay* out," she muttered, as she worked it down among the pebbles.

The day smelled of growing leaves and hot concrete, as always. So maybe last night was normal, and breezes often writhed in sheds, and this boundary was made of snail-shell hearts. Which meant people weren't telling her things, and maybe other secret boundaries looped the suburb. People did say bad weather usually went around, although death still got in.

In the kitchen, she knelt on her chair, elbows on the table, and flipped through an encyclopaedia. Her father had found an old set on a footpath, and expected her to use them instead of a computer. They weren't helping, but she suspected he'd disapprove of *River City Tombstones,* although it was by a professor.

"Stay home today," her father said, pouring coffee. "You have packed nothing."

"I don't want to move," she said. "What's *apotropaic?*"

"Look it up in the dictionary."

While she was getting it, she asked, "May I have a dog, please?"

"No."

She pulled a face over the book. A ghost dog wasn't really a dog.

"It's to guard against witches," she said.

"There is no such thing," her father said. "And we are moving—it is not time for a dog." And then, "Besides, that poor woman already has one."

"No, *apotropaic.* It means to protect against things." Like the snail shells. "Like mummifying cats in walls. They used to do that here."

Her father snorted, unsurprised. "What schoolwork is this?"

"Local history," she said, glibly. "I've changed my project."

"Good," said her father. They'd disagreed about notable local personages.

"Do you know any true scary stories about Bellworth? I only know our wallpaper, with the faces."

"If it's for school, you have to tell it yourself. But make it cheerful; there are plenty of bad things in the world without you adding more."

"Even here?" She reached for his plate.

"Yes, people who think they are cleverer than their fathers.

Drop that! You ate your breakfast. There are boxes in the hallway—pack your room."

"What if I *need* to know?"

"Why?" he asked, sharply. "Have you heard something? Seen something? Has someone done something to you?"

"No and no and no." It wasn't exactly a lie; if she said *yes,* he'd act, not answer.

"Stay inside, be good, don't trust neighbours," he said. "Don't take gifts. Be young while you can."

He was giving her a long peaceful childhood, and it felt like being wrapped in a blanket in the middle of summer, or staying too long at the bottom of the pool. But the truth would hurt him.

⁂

Grace's limbs no longer froze in place, and the new looseness frightened her. Pressure shifted behind one eye, soft petals pushing through. Her spine was ready to unfurl.

Tomorrow, Charlie had promised, but he slept late. Grace roamed the house, picked over the chocolates he'd left in the kitchen and finally broke into the locked room.

She went in through the wardrobe-space in Charlie's aunt's room. At the back, a panel slid open into another closet. She stumbled through a welter of shoes and dresses into a cool bedroom.

Ida's room, deadened by heat and time, had tasted of dust and mothballs; this was sweet as grapefruit and honeysuckle.

It was the opposite of Charlie's characterless verandah. Even Grace, with no memory of any age other than whatever she was now, saw this was a teenager's. The walls were duck-egg blue, and navy bamboo blinds striped the windows. Pastel bedding frothed around iron bed-ends garlanded with silk flowers, under a gauze canopy. On top of a bookcase, a few toys were set aside as carefully as childhood. But everywhere else was merry chaos. Posters of women—politicians and authors—were tacked to the wall, between art clipped from calendars. Cheap bright jewellery (a necklace of linked birds so cheap they must have meant something, a little aeroplane charm that turned like a promise between her fingers) swung from nails, knotted with hair-ribbons in institutional browns and golds—school colours. Shelves spilled CDs, nail polish, hand-annotated textbooks. A photocopied plastic-bound treatise on homesteads of South Gowburgh, labelled with a library sticker, slumped over a bangle enamelled with green flowers that caught the soft light. Grace tried to grow memories around each, but she had become too much herself.

There was no library of books on parasitic plants, no proof of unsavoury medical experiments by the family. Nothing to reveal why Grace's bones were bending like new twigs, or why she'd crawled uphill knowing only *Wren*. Not even evidence of extraordinary philanthropy.

Just the fragments of a person its occupant had been becoming, caught in amber. A shrine to a girl who had grown up.

On the desk, among exercise books, stood a photo: Cora in tartan and a school blazer, shaking hands with a woman in a vivid suit and a helmet of blond hair. Beside it, a certificate commended Cora Margaret Wren for bravery. A magazine article was tucked into an album: *Some sixteen-year-olds might have been traumatised by the experience. In spite of minor injuries, Cora Wren, pretty, witty, and sunny-natured, looks ahead to a bright future—*

Grace flipped forward. Between photographs and autographs were more clippings, equally enthused. She stopped on an inset picture: a group of children. The first was already indubitably Cora. The other was Charlie, but small, all teeth and elbows. Odd, to be able to see further into his past than her own. The third child was cropped out of the image, except for a round freckled arm.

She found no other pictures of that child, and few of Charlie. The album was about Cora: social sightings, news mentions, an announcement she would stand for council elections. A few letters of congratulations or invitation or compliment—*the sacrifices you've made, the cost . . .*

But those early clippings, Grace realised as she paged back, were also about Charlie.

. . . Dramatic ordeal—Cora Wren's selfless rescue of her young brother—fought off the attacker, who has not been identified—lucky to survive—the bravery we hope to see in a young leader in our community—it's dangerous in the creek, said another local girl, you never know what will grab you . . .

It was easy to imagine being saved by Cora—her bright face blurred by swirling silt, the strong sure hands. The vision rippled into a panicked memory of water pressing in—old information. Grace pushed it ruthlessly aside.

. . . Cora Wren, praised for rescuing her brother—a shallow grave already dug—rumoured disappearances—local man wanted for questioning . . .

If Wrens were habitually helpful, it explained why Grace came here, trusting Charlie to assist a stranger of whom he should have been wary. But the rest of the Wrens' clippings suggested the family was best at helping themselves.

. . . Brutal death of known character William Volney— assisting police in their enquires in relation to an assault foiled by local girl Cora Wren—foul play—insufficient evidence— "It's a friendly area, old-fashioned values—some families have lived here since there was *a here"—disappearances reported in Bellworth in the century and a half since its settlement by several English families—*

Only one hundred and fifty years. And no mention of the people there first, who had survived that settlement, or disappeared during it. Grace didn't imagine the arrival was amicable: the Wrens and their companions had inscribed their names too deeply over the suburb.

And yet she thought ferociously, one hundred and fifty years, a house and a name, a sister who rescued him, and what had Charlie made of it? How dared he have done nothing? If Grace could have slipped into his life, if this place were hers and—the image shoved her out. It reminded her too much of the grasping thing in the garden, the kick and resistance of the nothingness she'd swallowed.

She was Grace, for now, and she'd work out what that meant, or build a meaning, or die holding herself together.

⚜

The taxi driver's daughter needed information.

School was full of games of things-that-came-out-of-graves, or -the-night, or -the-creek. But the point was to not disturb the things in the first place, or else to run shrieking until home free. Both useless, when *things* turned out to be awake and in your street. To protect anyone against them, or to protect her particular dog phantom, she had to know more.

She strolled up to the graveyard, from where she could

watch both number 21 and her own driveway. Edith Tepping, weeding rosemary severely, said, "You should be at home."

"Yes," she answered, respectfully. "Are there ghosts here, Mrs Tepping?"

Mrs Tepping's face was like a slammed door. "You may disrespect your own ancestors," she said. "This is not a play-ground."

If Mrs Tepping, the oldest neighbour, wouldn't say, her only option was to ask the ghosts.

⌐◈⌐

Charlie slept in and dreamed hard—of deaths not quite his own, of being both the drowned and the hand forcing them down. Wonder, startlement, a departing mirror of air. When he woke, his nose and throat were roughened as if by dirty water, with a paint-stripping echo of gin. A dream-taste that belonged downstream.

In the midmorning light—white-green, amethyst—he sat up and scrubbed scabbed hands over his face. He concentrated on the building beneath and around him, invi-olate. The posts plunged into the earth, the roof rose to scrape against leaves.

And there was a noise that wasn't branches. Whisper-ings, as if a large moth were trapped in Cora's room.

"Grace?" he called.

The noises stopped.

He went into the hallway and rattled the crimped round handle. It was still locked.

"I went through the closets," said Grace, from Ida's door.

She had altered further in the night; her bones pressed differently against her skin. A stranger, and strange, and he'd turned her loose to rummage through the effects of a century and a half of Wrens, to siphon answers out of their hoarded secrets.

And Cora wanted her gone. Cora, who'd carried the scrapbooks away, as if they contained a scandal. As if family infamy wasn't as useful, these days, as fame.

The faster Grace found what she needed, Charlie reasoned, the better.

"They have Wren papers at the library," he said.

⚜

Ghosts, the taxi driver's daughter gathered, were usually summoned at night. But she was less likely to get caught by day.

When Mr Wren and the creek-woman left, she took her bag of supplies to number 21. Although the air pushed less against her when Mr Wren was gone, she stayed in the front garden in case she had to leave quickly.

The bees were loud—blue-banded and iridescent. She sat on the grass, and the warm affectionate breeze settled against her thigh.

"Who else is here?" she asked. No answer. The sun burned the backs of her arms, and it was hard to remember how scared she'd been in the shed.

"I brought you something," she said. "All-of-you." She addressed the yard at large, the shadows under the house, the glint of greenery behind. Then she wondered if the gesture was too broad.

"Anyway," she hurried on. "I want to know what's happening, and if somebody should do something." Sunlight fell on her knee like a dog resting its head. "Not," she added to it, "that anything's wrong with *you*. But I have to understand."

She set out two plastic bowls and continued. "I've made this up. Everything in books is . . . mirrors and candles and night, and blood and plan—planchettes, and I'd get in real trouble—and it didn't bring Mum home. We got a swamp-woman instead." She took two bottles from her bag and filled the bowls. "This one is milk—you've got to be hungry. In case you can't drink that, this is cordial, which is sugar and water and fruit. Ida gave it to us. I'm only allowed it on special occasions, and we never have those anymore. But it can't rot teeth if you don't have them."

She inhaled, steadied her nerves, then in one bowl she floated a cork with a needle in it. "We made a compass this way in science," she said. "Maybe some of you can move it, too."

She sat cross-legged, the bowls before her like drums. The ripples slowed. She saw her own milky reflection, a flock of honeyeaters tumbling overhead (sun fanning through green-stained wings), and once a little plane, although she didn't hear its engine over the bees. The light on her knee shifted with a silence like a sigh, but didn't move towards the bowls, and nothing else disturbed them.

Perhaps ghosts got self-conscious, too. Still, even in late morning, she didn't want to turn her back. The needle twisted idly. Her hair was hot with sun, and she had slept poorly. The scent of flowers was a blanket.

A sudden splash startled her upright. Magpies ascended from the roof.

On one bowl's brim, jewelled ants clustered. But in the other, the needle danced, and the cordial was fogged. As she watched, dirt sifted to the bottom. As if someone had trodden in it.

A bird crash-landing in the bowl, she told herself. A thin cloud slid over the sun, and she shivered. Silvered light weighted the grass, as if feet brushed the blades. The dog's warm presence was gone.

And what if it's not a dog? she thought, then wished she hadn't.

She emptied the bowls into the mouth of the drain beneath a downpipe. A flurry of bubbles that had once been ants rose, clinging, through the stagnant water.

⁂

After Charlie repaired the bicycle again, he and Grace wheeled it up through the cemetery.

She shook her head at the names. "Where did they bury Wrens before Bellworth?"

Charlie shrugged. "My aunt acted as if Gowburgh was founded on this graveyard. I mean, obviously there were Wrens before then. And graves. I don't suppose many family histories bear looking at too closely." He heard Cora in those words.

"I wish I had the chance to disagree with you," said Grace.

She looked well, in the sunshine among the headstones. Charlie told her about graveyard games. It sounded morbid, aloud. Grace said, *"Wrens."*

From there, Charlie loped alongside Grace, who, of all things, knew how to ride a bicycle. The triumph sustained her halfway. Then her face greyed. They unstrapped the milk crate and Grace, grudging, sat on the rear rack. Charlie, as he cycled, felt the corded leanness of her arms.

Although Ida was dead, and Cora wasn't there to disapprove, he was conscious he was making a spectacle of himself. Turning up Station Road, he almost tipped Grace onto the grass. He wanted to turn back, but Grace started laughing.

"*I* remembered how to ride," she said. Charlie grinned, and rode on.

The brick-and-timber library should have been replaced with something larger (an architectural horror, said Cora), but Bellworth had resisted. A plaque outside honoured a donation from a long-dead Damson-Wren. Grace mouthed the names on the notice board beside it. *Lost cockatiel. Answers to—*

Inside, Charlie asked the librarian, Joe Eising, about Wren papers.

"Those are in the State Library." He said it as if it were Charlie's fault—as if he found him an inferior Wren. "We don't have room for archives."

Charlie persevered. Local history? "Borrowed," said Joe. "What doesn't walk out." He carefully didn't look at Grace. Then, doubtful, "You could put a hold on them."

And leave a trail, Charlie thought. He was being paranoid. "I don't have a card. I'm leaving town soon." It sounded like a lie. "It's urgent."

The library computers were better than his phone. But neither he nor Grace, leaning over him (once or twice Charlie reached over his shoulder to push her upright), found anything useful.

"Let's go home," said Grace.

"One more thing." He searched for the City Hall exhibition Dr Anderton had despised.

Although it was long-closed, the website survived. The

screen blossomed, and for a moment, he hoped. But it didn't resolve into roses. Olive and gold figures, laurel and ivy—vintage curtains, the caption said. Except, somehow, in the style of it . . .

"Charlie," said Grace.

The exhibition had featured found works, collage, bricolage—even, disconcertingly, a few old pieces by Ida, representing *the endurance of the spirit*. An odd reminder that she'd been a successful artist, before she took reluctant charge of Charlie and Cora, before her health started failing. He skimmed the accompanying stories and reminiscences. Some sounded wholly invented. Girls who'd thrown cheap jewellery ("and at least once a diamond engagement ring") into a creek to appease or summon Dancing Jenny. A man trapped eternally on a train. An uncle whose plane had crashed in a rainforest, and when the sun slanted just right it might still be seen—rust-roughened and greened by vines—sliding sugar-slow on the air.

"This one's by another Kenton," he said quietly. "Listen. *'My great-grandfather learned, at war'*—"

"*Charlie!*" said Grace. He turned, and saw her face.

Light caught on her lower lip as if something sharp pressed up through it. She clutched her eye, as if against pain.

Ghosts could wait.

But outside on the footpath, Mrs Braithe rested meaningly on her walking stick, her grocery bag by her feet. She eyed him up and down. "You're not eating properly."

"Thank you for the—" Charlie scrabbled for details "—the grapefruit, Mrs Braithe."

"We welcomed a young Wren in the street," she said sharply. "But no one wants trouble. Your aunt kept to herself.

Your sister understands how to run matters." Her gaze darted past him, flinched from Grace. "Keep things in check." Her hand twitched towards her chest. *She's afraid,* Liddy had said.

"The Wrens," she added, "have always been respectable."

"Of course, Mrs Braithe," said Charlie. "I'm here to tidy up."

"Good," said Mrs Braithe. She lifted her bag before he could offer, and stalked away.

Charlie watched her out of earshot, then asked, to ease the mood, "Do you think we have been, though? Respectable?"

But Grace said, "Something doesn't want me here."

Then she dropped. Charlie, catching handfuls of her shirt, dragged her to a bench. He propped her up straight.

"Hold it together," he begged. Her spine felt wrong, as if what kept her in the shape of a body was softer than twigs and branches. How far had the roses spilled? "You need—" He didn't know. Water? A doctor? "Grace—*Grace.*" One eye was widening blue. The beds of her fingernails blossomed in bruises.

"Stop," he hissed. As if flowers listened.

He glanced frantically around. The shop windows were opaque with reflections. In the library's garden, a currawong, bright-eyed, cocked its head. Storm drains breathed out the scent of the creek. "I'll get you something to eat," he said. "Or drink, or—"

"I'm not this." Grace's voice was leaf-thickened. "I'm not the dead—"

Two police officers stepped from the café opposite.

Charlie was worried less about them than about new-made ghosts, the remnants of old ones. Was something quieter than a shadow blossoming from the grating, following the police as they crossed the road?

We haven't looked far enough back, he was about to say to Grace. *You're right—you aren't the dead, we should be asking* them.

"Charles Matthew Wren," said the older of the officers. Charlie recognised him—he wasn't local. "What's going on here?"

He had nothing to hide—or nothing they suspected him of. But Cora would hear, and he couldn't risk Grace. If he got her to number 21, surely she'd recover.

Yes, this was his housemate. No, she wasn't drunk, wasn't on drugs; it was food poisoning. Yes, his sister knew about her. No, he still hadn't heard from Alli Kenton. Yes, he'd been out with his sister the night before, and then home. Grace saw him. Had something happened? No? Might they go?

If it hadn't been for Grace, he wouldn't have accepted a lift from the police. If not for Cora's connections, he doubted they would have offered.

Grace steadied as they drew closer to the house, although she kept her face turned to the passing suburb. Flame trees and bougainvillea and chickens in the yard of the manse. They passed the entrance to Volney Street twice before Charlie pointed it out. Grace limped through the gate unassisted.

"If you were going to hurt me, what help would they give?" she asked, weakly.

Charlie frowned as the police car pulled away. "Maybe they think you're safe, now I know they're watching."

WINDOWS

My great-aunt (says one of the tradies from across the oval) re-fused to buy things secondhand, even when times were tight. "You don't know what's living in them," she'd say.

Her husband was the opposite. He'd bring home chairs he found along the road, but my great-aunt wouldn't use them—she said they felt crowded. He picked up a lovely long ladder, pre-used, just right for the gutters. My great-aunt said he ought to have asked why it was being sold. She made him get rid of it after he put it up outside her sewing room window and wandered off. She saw (she swore) someone come down it who wasn't her husband.

The last straw was when he found a set of leadlight win-dows, perfect for enclosing a verandah. "What happened to the house they came from?" she demanded.

Still, in they went—amber, bottle blue, sea green. But when storms rolled in (all the same colours), my great-aunt felt watched. One night the power went out. She heard water roaring, and made her husband search for an open window, but on the ve-randah, they both froze. Although the house was high set, waves rushed past. Lightning flashed on faces shouting soundlessly; drowning-pale hands clawed at the glass as they swept by.

Her husband tried to pull the people inside. But my great-aunt packed her bags. She left him and moved in with my gran and stayed there until she died.

CHAPTER FOURTEEN

Beneath

The house was not empty. Grace, first through the gate, felt it: a presence of sun and soap.

"Cora's here," said Charlie. His hand snagged on her thorny shoulder, and he snatched it clear, then shepherded her down the side, ignored by birds. The air clung and parted like rotting cloth.

Although the front verandah was head-height, the block sloped, so that the kitchen was much higher set. Beneath it, in a corner loosely enclosed by palings, a rough slab had been poured. A nest of pipes clung to the underneath of the kitchen floor, and descended to an aged washing machine and a cement sink.

"Stay here," said Charlie. "I'll talk to her."

The rest of the space beneath number 21, open-slatted on all sides, was a labyrinth. The tangle was densest at the centre, which Grace guessed was below the fireplace. Around it, clouded light silhouetted skeletal furniture. A canoe, long as a crocodile, hung over stacked green louvres and wine-coloured panes. An ancient tricycle crouched, insectile, atop a pyramid of plastic and plywood crates.

"Cora has met me," Grace reminded him, annoyed. They were losing time; she hated her helplessness, her willingness to grasp at any hope Charlie dangled, the fact she'd lain awake the night before, barricaded in the parlour, until he returned. "Why do you have to hide me?"

"I'm not," he whispered. "I let Cora think you'd be leaving, and she expects the world to go the way she plans."

Cora liked *me*, Grace thought. She said, "What will she do?"

"Sigh at me," said Charlie, exasperated. "Will you stay here for a few minutes? You're okay, aren't you? Let me see—"

It was not that Charlie's touch was possessive. Grace was used to it, and he turned her face to examine her neck with the casualness of habit. But when he'd supported her outside the library, his fingers had crinkled her skull as if it were paperbark. When he'd steadied her out of the police car, the vines beneath her skin and shirt had recoiled against his hand. Now, if his thumb under her chin pressed a little harder . . .

She pulled away and stood against a post. "I'm better," she lied.

Soon he'd discover she was as breakable as her attacker. She'd fall apart, fluted and hollow like a paper-wasp nest, her terrors buzzing away. No more Grace to care there was no more Grace. No crime. No loss. No *thing*.

She wanted to say something true. "It—I—was wrong there, at the library, the shops." The atmosphere had been too thin, so far from Volney Street; her strength had drained away, leaving only a brittle residue of fears, and she'd been forced to rely on him.

"Did you remember anything?" asked Charlie. As if she hadn't nearly crumbled on the footpath. As if she wasn't trapped here.

This house and this Wren might keep her in one piece, but she refused to be grateful. Not when she'd arrived furious to live. Not when Charlie, around whom suspicions crowded like moths at a window, was so unstartled by her dissolution.

"Nothing," she said. Only the certainty of being leaf-mould and mud, a miasma of grief she wouldn't own. "Go inside. I'll search here." Then, mocking, "Tell me when it's safe."

⁂

Charlie did not want to abandon Grace. But whatever she was, whatever had come after her in the dark, she had survived so far. And today, he sensed the garden growing, blue-glossed crows lifting towards the full sky (rain would come soon, not yet). It was easy not to worry.

And if there *was* cause to doubt her ... In Charlie's experience, suspicions rarely went unpursued. They only needed to wait and see what else came after Grace.

He circled to the front again, through the fringed fern-and-loquat jungle along the side fence (as a boy he'd climbed through a gap there, but it had long since been repaired from the neighbour's garden). Sunlight, scented with lemon myrtle, rolled past him up the steps and through the open doors.

For a moment, he imagined a daylit construct, an avenging spirit of hot flowers and birdsong, scouring Aunt Ida's house.

It was Cora. She was in her old room, looking what Aunt Ida had called *put-together*. Her uncreased clothes gleamed against the room's blue walls, the preserved memories of youth.

"Student leader!" she said. She angled a pin on a school tie, throwing reflections in Charlie's eyes. "I should leave this room for future biographers. Schoolkids already want to interview me."

If she kicked off her heels, she'd be the same height as that long-ago Cora—the one who'd chafed at childhood. Otherwise, she was unrecognisable. She'd got hold of her own life, and well-being and will shone from her like a candle.

Charlie supposed that happened when you worked out what to be—even if that was only a local councillor.

It was the first time he had thought "only" about Cora.

Still, certainties were worth protecting. He was glad Grace was downstairs, as if the contrast would reveal her as a trick of the eye. Shadows of branches.

"Ida threw out everything of mine," he said. Cora looked sympathetic, which had not been his intention.

"Well, unlike her, you have your health. And all this."

She tossed the tie onto the desk, brushed past him, put her back to the wall across the hallway, grinned, and pushed open the hidden door.

Always outdoors, hating the house, leaving as soon as he could, Charlie had forgotten this direct path to the parlour. The door, of the same jointed boards as the wall, was hinged on the inside. It swung into a high-ceilinged closet space, narrow and dark. It held a second fireplace and a dusty shudder of old dread borrowed from a story—Ida's or Cora's. Its walls should have been scratched by fingernails.

Cora opened the opposite door. There was Grace's sofa with its slipping springs, the blank stares of dead Wrens. Some of them had seen the house hauled uphill to its present location, the walls rearranged.

Cora sat. Charlie bundled up the crocheted blankets in which Grace had slept, if sleep was the right word. A few brittle twigs fell out and his sister picked them up idly, crumbled them. Then she looked at the haphazard encyclopaedias, touched the circles the mugs had left on the coffee table, and her brow furrowed.

Charlie needed to leave Gowburgh for Cora's sake, as much as his own. She invested half her energy in him, and he repaid her with worry.

"This will go faster if we hire a skip," he said.

"Stop looming," said Cora. "Sit."

He didn't. He'd have to flounder out of the armchairs, and she would, of course, offer a hand.

"Charlie! What's going on?"

Cora solved problems, made the ephemeral vanish. He should tell her and be glad.

"Ghosts," he bit out. "Cora, don't laugh yet." What explanation was there? The depth of the creek's silence, the reflections cast by birds he couldn't see, the tangible currents of the air . . .

"Things have been weird," he said. "Grace—"

Cora sighed.

"Grace is sick! It's as if her tattoos are growing. People talk about hauntings. I keep smelling Dennis—"

"Who?" said Cora. "Oh, the dog." Cora and Dennis had never been fond of each other.

"Then a—a *thing* came out of the garden. Like a scarecrow, but walking." He steeled himself to say casually, as if his arms didn't remember the impact, "I hit it with a shovel and it fell apart." And today, he was being watched from gutters.

In the face of Cora's amused doubt, he kept on. "What

if what's happening to Grace took Alli? I know it sounds unlikely—"

"Charlie, calm down."

"You don't believe me." He hadn't expected her to, but he deserved some reward for having told her.

"I don't deal in things I can't touch," said Cora. "That doesn't mean they're not there. But mysteries are like mould; a little sunlight cures them." It might have been a line from one of her speeches. "Show me where you saw this scarecrow."

                    ⚬⚬⚬

The shadows below the house were damp, the algae-stained stumps submarine. Overhead, timbers creaked—the building in restless conversation with its inhabitants.

Rest had only ever brought Grace a new stage of decay, so instead she waded into the depths. From a shoebox, an eyeless doll stared, hair brittle on its celluloid skull; it reminded her of herself. A chest of silverware, incomplete—had she eaten with it, or done harm? A thickening tendril of recollection told her she had done terrible things to survive. Some part of Grace knew the names of well-worn tools: wood-planes and shoe-lasts. A mangle, a canvas curtain.

She lifted that. Behind was a wall deep as it was wide—stone, then brick, set with shallow arches almost like doors. The foundation of the fireplace, Grace realised. Her fingertips caught on pick-marks and scratched names—Wren children, she supposed.

Down by the creek, becoming herself, she had seen something similar, a broken wall graffitied, tented with branches. And before? She squeezed her eyes shut until light blossomed, then pushed through it. Memories skittered, fragmenting nightmarishly. Reality was the circling carvings, her skin shrinking over sinews. Her lips drew away from too-sharp teeth. Her reason eroded—

Velvet legs feathered over her shoulders. Grace snapped into herself too late. They scurried under her collar and *inside her chest.*

Fury rushed back to Grace. She scrabbled at her shirt-collar, ready to rip herself open to tear the intruder out. But it hadn't been prepared to find her inhabited. It spasmed, crumbled, and dissolved into dust and patience, and Grace—

"Are you dead?"

She opened her eyes. The underhouse was luminous, the snarled pipes swung, and the laundry floor was cold under her. She tried to remember returning there. Scrambling.

A girl frowned, upside down, her narrow face for a moment glancingly familiar. "You nearly ran me over, and you've cut yourself. Here." She turned away.

Grace groaned, and pulled herself up the thirsty concrete of the laundry sink. Spongey skin was stripped from one palm, rasped from her knuckles. She ran them under the tap, and pretended she'd seen blood. The pebbled basin looked cool with moss, or mould. She wanted to put her head down and let the stream soften the thickening mass behind her skull. Wanted, too, to flee from water—a new distaste, jostling into place.

Stay Grace.

The girl dragged over a storage bag and tugged out cloth—a bedspread dripping lace daisies, then a faded pillowcase once garish with orange leaves. She tore a strip from it. "For your hand."

The green dress Grace had first worn hung on the side of the sink. She blotted the abrasions with it. Memories tried to anchor to the cloth, and fell apart—she saw now how worn it was, how frayed the green embroidered flowers around the neck. It should have been thrown away. Then she bandaged her hand.

"You were grabbing your neck," said the girl. "As if you'd been poisoned." She held up more cloth. "It's all scraped."

"Why are you here?" asked Grace.

"Hiding," said the girl. "I'm allowed here! Miss Wren *said*. But I didn't want her to see me."

"Why not?" Grace gingerly wrapped her throat.

The girl made a face, and gestured. Her sneakers had no laces, and she'd trodden down the heels; her much-worn shorts and t-shirt were far too large.

"Ah," said Grace. She, too, felt shabby beside Cora.

"Do you want a mint? I'm not allowed gum." And when Grace shook her head, the girl suggested, "Put the knot on one side. My mum said that was stylish."

Grace laughed, coughed, obeyed, and buttoned her collar over her newest repair.

The girl looked affronted, then pleased. "And since Mr Wren would yell, I was going to sneak out."

"You'd better," said Grace. Children meant noise and stones, but she liked this one. Having no history, she already felt as if they'd known each other for days. "It isn't safe."

"I *know*!" said the girl, so hungrily that Grace jerked away. "I have *hundreds* of questions. What are your tattoos, and can I take my mum's dress, and what was the—"

The back door opened. They froze—there were voices above.

Grace had questions, too, but a child wasn't likely to have answers. "Go!"

The girl seized the dress from the sink, and rustled through the papyrus grass under the stairs. Moments later, the front gate sang.

Charlie trod warningly down the steps. His sister's feet in grass-green shoes, her flared skirt brilliant with flowers, followed.

Grace, borrowing caution from the thing that had most recently, so briefly, possessed her, slunk into shadow.

⚜

Charlie expected to see only dry leaves in the grass. But something shuffled inside the shed, batted blunt and urgent against the wired window. *Let it be a bird*, he thought.

Before he could warn Cora, she unlatched the door.

It wasn't a bird.

Overnight, Grace's attacker had put itself back together. It had built a body of paper and torn dog-food bags, vines that had crept under the walls to die, a sheen of shed snakeskin.

The figure reeled in the sudden light. Then, staggering, it crashed and fell among paint cans and hoses.

In full day, it was harder to accept its existence. The intensity with which it had lunged at Grace was gone. Now it huddled, abject, and Charlie pitied it. He waited for his sister to say—anything.

"Pass me the rake," said Cora. Not horrified. Intrigued.

She waved the rake over the whatever-it-was, looking for strings. It flinched in the dust, although it had no eyes, just hollows in which shadows dipped and bulged. Cora prodded it with the tines. Not gently.

The creature rattled. Nubs of fingers (or toes) clenched at the handle, not catching hold.

"It went for Grace," said Charlie. He meant it as a warning, but heard himself pleading. Repulsion mingled with sick guilt, and for its own sake, as much as his, he wanted this to be the being he had struck down.

"We're safe enough," said Cora, cheerfully. She settled the rake onto the papery thorax. "We've dealt with worse."

A thin limb lashed towards Charlie, who sidestepped. Cora put her foot on its wrist, flattening it as if it were cardboard.

"It likes you," said Cora. Too calm.

The thing convulsed, tearing under Cora's green shoe, but it did not rip free. Charlie wondered how painstakingly it had formed this second body.

"So," said Cora. "What's the game?"

"*I* don't know," said Charlie.

She rolled her eyes, passed him the rake, and moved her foot. The creature pulled back against itself, miming pain.

"It's cleverly made," said Cora. "Is one of your friends behind this?"

Alli? he wondered, then realised Cora assumed this was a trick. She'd dragged him to theatre events at which she was a guest, and he dimly recalled discussions of fake blood, lyrical marionette demonstrations, performers—muscular, anxious, on the point of being lost. Some of them had been.

"It's not a puppet," he said. "It's a—a shell."

Cora leaned down, curiosity flickering like hunger. The thing cringed. Its face looked like someone gasping through wet cloth. Cora touched it.

Her slim hand, weighted with Aunt Ida's blue-black sapphire, rested on its chest. It clutched at her with an un-injured arm; she caught hold, and peeled snakeskin from whip-cord vines. *It's just a thing,* he reminded himself. Its skin, apart from the scales, was as fragile as Grace's.

"Cora—"

"This is well done." She straightened and retrieved the pruning secateurs.

"What are you doing?"

She knelt, her skirt a pooled garden. "Seeing how it works."

"Don't," said Charlie.

"Don't you want answers?"

She always did. Liddy would have. Grace was ransacking the house from curiosity. But Charlie hadn't planned how to explain what he felt, seeing iron bite into what wasn't flesh.

"Leave it alone," he said. "You're right. It's someone's joke. That horrible girl, maybe—I don't know why Ida let her keep her projects in here."

"Have you seen her recently?" asked Cora.

"I warned her away." The figure had fallen too lightly to be a person in disguise.

"Oh, Charlie. Aren't you even a bit curious?"

Cora's certainties underpinned Charlie's life. If there was something she didn't know, he was free to make his own mistakes.

"I don't need trouble," he said, stiffly. "It's a practical joke, but it had a scrap of Alli's scarf, and if someone's willing to joke that way . . . The police were here once today."

"Already?" Cora said, genuinely surprised. Curiosity gone, she stood. The thing was scarcely moving.

"It was probably that kid's revenge for not letting her run wild," he said. "Look, it's wound down. I'll bury it in the garden."

"Do that," said Cora. Something slithered in the dirt. She put her shoe on it, twisted, then smiled. "No other ghosts before I leave?"

"I'm sorry," said Charlie. "It's nerves. Everything. Being here alone."

"Except for Grace," said Cora.

She already wore her civic face, vibrant and efficient. She had meetings to attend, police contacts to speak to; she was returning to the business of calling the city's tune. For a moment Charlie, who owed Cora everything, *wanted* to complicate her grown-up life. He wanted to march his sister to Grace, force her to grasp that knuckled wickerwork, brush skin like swollen pages, and admit aloud that something wasn't right.

Outside the shed, she reached to pat his shoulder. "When you were little, you wanted faraway wonders. Then Alli made you dissatisfied all over again. But look."

She gestured to the silvering house, the pierced awnings over back windows, the breeze-ruffled texture of glass. Tree-wreathed, bird-haunted, so deep-set in Bellworth he could no longer imagine climbing out.

"You don't appreciate what we have here," she said.

MOTEL

There used to be a motel in Greenstone (says Cherie, Edith Tepping's granddaughter). It was on the other side of the highway, before there was one. I'd run deliveries up to it, and a man always sat in a folding chair in front of the room nearest the office, breathing diesel fumes from trucks on the overworked roads. A big man, at his ease. When I'd passed an accident on the way—and that wasn't uncommon—he knew about it and wanted to hear the details. His eyes would light up like he'd seen dinner brought in.

Then they put the highway through—skimming the edge of Bellworth, cutting into Greenstone. Saving time, saving lives. The old road got orphaned, broken apart. It's still there: fragments creeping along the chainmesh fencing, dead ends cradling the husks of service stations, cracked pavement turned into parking lots for rusted-out prime movers.

One night recently the creek was high, and I had to rat-run through the maze of cut-off streets in Greenstone to get home. I passed the old Motor Inn, abandoned years ago. But for a moment as I drove by, I could have sworn someone was sitting outside one of the rooms. A gaunt man grinning out at the dark, waiting for an accident on that deserted road.

CHAPTER FIFTEEN

Advice

When the Wrens had gone upstairs—Charlie slouched under his height, Cora exactly as she ought to be—Grace slipped from beneath the house.

Sunlight sank into her bones, strong as honey. She wanted to luxuriate on the hot grass. Then for the first time, she saw one of the invisible presences—a glassy ripple of air seeping from the shed.

It shimmered through the grass and nosed, weakening, towards the steps. Before it reached her, it blew away on a breeze. *Good,* she thought. For its sake.

Charlie mustn't have even tried to explain to his sister. If he had, Cora—who was obviously the sort of person who put things right—couldn't have left the shed smiling.

But it wasn't clear either Wren believed an orderly world had room for things like Grace. Charlie had said, matter-of-factly, he planned to bury something in the backyard.

She crossed to the shed and looked in.

On the floor, a broken husk fluttered. Strength trickled out, shivering the dust.

Charlie arrived beside her, alone. "It's wounded," he said. "It's dying."

"It attacked you," he reminded her. He was carrying the torn bag of linens.

"It was trying to survive." The thing had burrowed into her, hungry, and she was sorry for what she saw of herself in it. And afraid.

Charlie shook a stained blanket out over the figure. Doubly faceless, it plucked at the tartan from below. Muffled, it could suffocate or be beaten to stillness. Or set on fire—unremarkable in a yard this large.

Charlie stepped forward, and Grace seized his arm. "Don't hurt it!"

Buried, that last sliver of life crushed away from the day—

"I won't," said Charlie. "I didn't mean to, this time."

He dropped his gaze to her bandaged hand, but she didn't let go, and when he knelt, Grace followed. He folded the blanket into a pathetic parcel. If he put it out with the rubbish, to be compacted . . .

"Hey!" Charlie snapped his fingers in front of her eyes. "Come back."

Grace shook her head clear. She was imagining too many deaths for anyone to have survived them all.

"I'm taking it to Liddy," he said. "She'll have to help now."

Grace let go, and he wrapped garden twine around an object too small to be a body, then stood, cradling it in one arm.

"Keep looking while you can," he sighed. "You might still find an answer."

Maybe she would decompose cleanly in the grass, leaving nothing to be carted away. Perhaps there had been nothing to learn except this: she, like it, was merely another stirring of river-wrack washed into this stagnant yard, with its tidemarks of souls.

"No," she said, but Charlie was already gone.

～☙～

Something was happening in number 21, where the Wrens had so much history they piled it up and forgot it. The taxi driver's daughter burned with curiosity and envy.

She and her dad didn't own anything much older than herself: a pretty faceted biscuit tin from Ida her mother hadn't lived long enough to return, and which now held small treasures; their house itself with its old carpets and creepy wallpapers, which her dad had halfheartedly tried to replace before selling. He'd even finally removed the bathroom wallpaper her mother had hated: a pattern of watchful faces. Until he painted the wall, that had only made the creepiness worse—as if the watchers had simply turned invisible.

But fixing that hadn't brought her mother back, any more than the message for the not-a-witch. Any more than brides ever came home in her aunt's legends of women who flew away when their husbands didn't listen.

Her mother, it turned out, had been right. But she was still dead.

When Cora, and then Mr Wren, and then—limping furtively—Grace left number 21, the taxi driver's daughter was watching from her own living room, nose pressed against the orange glass.

～☙～

Whatever everyday marvels Cora accused Charlie of ignoring, the thing in his arms was real. No heavier than vines and paper, but as genuine as his water-map of the city. Solid as Grace's roses.

After Cora left, until he saw Grace creep towards the shed, he'd stood at the kitchen sink and stared through the little avocado sapling—still alive, after its misadventure, rootlets webbing the jar. He'd imagined, too vividly, the *thing* in a rubbish bag, its indistinct mouth gaping against taut plastic.

What if Grace's problem was infectious, and what he was carrying down the street now had been a person, full of vigour and opinions? (Not Alli—surely a person couldn't become this so quickly.) What if his own scratches were already seeded with unfurling greenery?

A terrible thought, yet not the worst.

The sailboat wheel in the Eisings' yard accelerated, then ran out of wind. A butcherbird opened its beak soundlessly, as if swallowing air. Under his foot, a seedpod cracked; a porcelain snap echoed from a garden.

He entered the ghostly water with relief, stepped over the low log fence into the reserve, trod sideways downhill among blue-tufted weeds.

On the path to Liddy's, he ignored the breeze rustling the frameworks. Stick figures did not turn to watch. He only imagined a breathy voice pursuing. The bundle stirred less and less. When he reached the makeshift causeway, the blanket had stilled. He crossed alone except for his own thin reflection.

Behind the dead house, casuarinas whispered, hung with chimes—keys and beads and bolts, something glinting like a wedding ring. A shred of blue tarp, corrugated tin between the branches—

Charlie forgot the dog until it flashed growling through striated shadows.

"Liddy!" he shouted, holding the parcel high.

She appeared, reassuringly sturdy, but didn't call back the animal. "Go away. Volney Street and its concerns can drown together." She struck her forehead. "I forgot—you're a Wren. You don't care what I say."

"Something needs your help," said Charlie. The dog circled, sinuous.

"Not my problem," said Liddy. "I'm busy." She turned away.

"You're the one person who understands!" exclaimed Charlie. "And—and Liddy, I don't want to have killed it!"

She faced him again, fists on hips. Warily watching the dog, Charlie lowered the blanket to the ground and unwrapped it. The papier-mâché head was dented in; the flaking skin undulated, as if with faint breathing. Vines spilled across the tartan.

"I certainly didn't make *this*!" said Liddy. She squatted and knocked on the skull. "Hollow."

"Don't—"

"Afraid it will bite me?" asked Liddy, and looked up. "Or that I'll bite it?"

"It's injured, Liddy."

"It's not alive."

Charlie crossed his arms more tightly. "I'd rather assume it is, than—" Than kill it twice? Than be so cavalier with a life?

Liddy waved him aside. "This head's been made on purpose," she said. "By Ida?"

"A kid," he said. "I think Ida taught her."

"There's a thought." His aunt hadn't cared for Liddy, either. "What was she up to? It's good work, though. I wonder who it was meant to be."

"Your scarecrows—" began Charlie.

"—were *meant* as scarecrows. Or decoys, or lures—I've heard different stories, and some have been here a long time. Wind-haunts, Bill called them. But this feels like a cage." She rocked onto her heels, with an expression he remembered her saving for homework. "I don't know, Charlie! Nobody taught me anything and the price of *understanding*? I've figured some things out, I've strained off stuff washing in from over-the-creek, the bits of stories people tell when they beg for advice. From *me*."

She dragged her hands over her face, pushed back her rusty hair. "The pieces don't make a picture. Just . . . glimpses, gossip. And they expect me to fix their filthiest problems." She shook her head, hardened again. "What happened?"

He described ambush, dissolution, rediscovery. He left out Cora's callousness. "If it's a person—"

"It's not," said Liddy. "Or that's leaked away."

Her examination was brisk, but not careless. Charlie winced as she traced the perforations left by the rake. Then she looped back her faded hair, pressed her ear to the sunken chest, straightened, and said, "Stay here."

The dog kept its golden gaze fixed on him until Liddy returned. "Open that," she said, and tossed a small box of milk at Charlie.

Tearing off the corner, he cut his finger on the foil.

Liddy took hold of the box and his hand, pulled him down to kneel on the blanket, and pressed a smear of blood into the carton. "Better you than me." She grinned.

Charlie knew that glint. When they were kids, she'd left fruit out for possums, seed for parrots. "Are you sure you want to feed—"

"I'm not sure about anything," said Liddy. "I want to *know*."

The mouth did not, of course, open. Liddy poured bloodied milk into the collapsing chest. It seeped through, darkening. She rubbed her hands in the dirt, as deliberately as a surgeon washing before a procedure. Then she eased her fingers through the separating skin, felt around, and ripped out—*something*.

It was soft and palely translucent. Glassy fibres stretched and trembled, wet and white as the roots of waterweeds.

The softening remains on the blanket crumpled inward; something hitched in Charlie's chest. "You've killed it!"

"This?" Liddy held up her trophy. "This isn't life. At most, it's a—a channel, a conduit for something. I've seen it before. I told you, things are getting worse, and people have noticed—the fences and chimes aren't all mine. Deaths are choking the creeks, catching in this. It's grown through the channel, through the dirt. Now it's crawling into shells."

"Or they're forming around it," said Charlie.

Liddy looked at him sharply, then shook the writhing web, already dried almost transparent. "I pull out what I find, but it comes back. Faster, lately."

Charlie reached out, and Liddy slapped his hand. She produced a lighter from her skirt pocket, struck a flame, and held it to the filaments.

They flared in a smokeless lace of fire, and were gone.

"That seemed easy," Charlie said. His veins crawled.

"That was a hungry, shrivelled scrap of it. But it's solved *your* problem."

She scuffled professionally through the remains on the

blanket. A spiralled seedpod, straw-blond. The fish-scale glint of sequins. Lined paper, tight-folded into a damp pellet.

Give it to me, he wanted to say. *I caught it, so what's inside is mine.*

To buy time, he asked, "Liddy, isn't there anyone else who might know what's going on, and help us?"

"No," said Liddy, flatly. "Not about this. Or if I've asked, they agree Bellworth should deal with its own messes."

He wanted to snatch the paper out of her hand. He'd burn it, and no one would know whose handwriting was on the note, or whose name. But Grace needed the truth.

Liddy prised it open. "The ink's washed out," she said. "Gifts and glass and bird's nests are proper hearts for a scarecrow." (*And dead roots,* thought Charlie.) "This is rubbish."

"Maybe that's all it had," said Charlie.

They knelt, silent. Wind hissed in the trees, settled. The chimes behind the house rang a second too late.

"Aren't you ever afraid, out here alone?" Charlie asked.

The moment had passed. "Should I be?"

"I meant—" He stumbled. Ghosts. Unsolved murders. Desperate strangers.

Liddy, more exasperated than hateful, said, "I'll give you this for free. Every suburb is peculiar. But people out of Bellworth? I've been connecting their stories, and no, they don't make sense, but it's been like—like sticking petals onto a flower, or repairing an eggshell. There's a big empty space in the middle. And in *that,* there's plenty of room for Volney Street. And for the Wrens, who've never done badly out of events."

"I was nearly killed!" said Charlie. "I haven't hurt anyone." He wished the words back.

"Have you saved anyone?" asked Liddy.

"That's unfair." Charlie stood. "Have you? Yesterday you said a little power needs a big sacrifice. Well, the most I can do is guess where the creek has flowed. I can't help *death* being clogged. We've been here since the beginning—"

Liddy, still seated, scoffed.

"—of *Bellworth*," he continued. "So if I should be surprised my family shows up in stories, or believe being attacked gives me some special responsibility to stop it happening to other people—"

"Maybe all I mean is you're too comfortable," said Liddy.

In the trees, bits of things newly visible clung leechlike to Grace's clothes, swam hungering through the branches. When she climbed the fence, she left strands of her thoughts, herself, trailing from it. The crossing was syrupy with reaching reflections.

Watching from the casuarinas, she waited to follow Charlie back, for fear of losing herself in the creek's flashing shadows. But when he was out of hearing, Liddy said, flatly, "You must be Grace."

Grace emerged. Liddy folded the blanket and stood. "It's meant to be hard for people to get here at the same time," she added. "Safer, that way."

Her square face echoed in Grace's mind, as though seen through water. If Liddy was startled by Grace's appearance, she didn't show it.

"I didn't want Charlie to kill the—the thing, " Grace explained.

Watching Liddy grasp those cancerous tendrils, she had

too easily imagined them coiling through her veins. The roses were part of herself, but those fibres had their own groping, feeding existence. Grace wanted to claw her chest open. Instead, she clasped her hands; her knuckles pressed through her skin.

"You're a fine pair," said Liddy. "And now?"

Grace hesitated, then fumbled with the knotted cloth around her throat.

"Only Charlie has seen this," she said. "If you know what it is—"

"I don't," said Liddy, but strode forward and tugged at the layers of Grace's collars, to see. Her blunt hands traced the woven roses, the cracked bark thickening Grace's shoulder. "Another piece that makes no sense," she said.

"I'm not like that thing, am I?" said Grace.

"You're a whole jungle," said Liddy. She turned Grace's head to look first in the direction of the dead house, then away.

"But I have seen you," Liddy went on. "In puddles in the reeds. You've been stealing faces from reflections—I can't say you've improved on them. You're not one of those scarecrows. Something new—maybe branches washed together to look human enough. Empty places suck things into them."

"I'm a person," said Grace. The problem was that things were trying to get the life *out* of her. "I couldn't want to live so much if I wasn't. I know words, names, how to ride a bike!"

"There's no blood under your skin, though," replied Liddy. "Your eyes are the ideas of eyes—too many layered over each other." She held Grace's face still. "A rose is growing through one—had you noticed? You might be new, but you're falling apart."

"And do I have those roots, too?" asked Grace bitterly. "Are you going to rip them out and burn them?"

"Do you want me to?"

For all she knew, they held her together. "I want to survive."

"Everyone wants that." Liddy let go. "Nobody gets to." She sounded abruptly uncertain.

"The first thing I remembered was *Wrens*," pleaded Grace. "I went straight to their house. It must mean something."

"It means you looked for trouble."

"Then the Wrens *are* involved."

"Or careless." Liddy's gaze shifted into the distance, then snapped back. "Not that I'd threaten one. But if Wrens can't take care of the Wrens, I don't see why anyone else should. Look out for yourself."

Grace had to know. "Can I trust Charlie?"

A corner of Liddy's mouth tucked down, sourly. "You can't blame rotten wood for breaking." That wasn't a *no*. Liddy continued. "I spent too much time with Wrens once, and see what happened to me."

Liddy was weathered and alive. She had answers (a few), and a secret island between suburbs for herself, and a striped dog yawning sharp-toothed at her feet.

"What did happen?" asked Grace.

❧

You won't believe Charlie's my age (said Liddy, settling on the dry grass). Mrs Braithe's mother used to say the Wrens hadn't arrived *respectably*—they'd simply outlived anyone who knew otherwise. But Charlie and Cora moved here with their mother.

When she died, old Ida kept them. I lived down the street, and the trouble we got into! Not Cora, of course—Charlie and I, we had fun. The things we convinced each other we saw . . . Yet our families had been here so long, it was as if someone bigger was breathing all the air. Too much history. Charlie and I planned to leave, see the world and stay kids forever. But you don't get to choose when to grow up.

Old Bill Volney lived here, then—in that house behind me. And not so old that he'd made plans for dying. He did what I do, listening to questions, guessing answers, and people muttered about him, same as about me. He was the suspect in that fuss about Charlie, and Cora's heroics. And afterwards it felt, like rising water, that Bellworth wanted him gone. You'd see him, and taste bile behind your teeth. You'd find you had a rock in your hand.

It wasn't the first or last time a mood took the place. It even got to me, and I knew he was innocent. He was there the day Charlie fell in the creek, but as I told anyone who'd listen, he was helping. That's usually a mistake.

I wasn't in at the kill. I'd been sent to my room, and from the window I saw people slipping through the moon-light, down to the creek. When I climbed out, my parents caught me.

The next morning, Bill was dead in a pool of blood. And that left a pit—a sinkhole—in the world. He'd held part of it together, and suddenly jobs weren't getting done, and people started seeing uncomfortable things. Plenty of night-mares, too, although those could have another explanation.

But that gap needed a person to fill it. Maybe it chose me because I'd stood up for him. I've learned my lesson.

At first, I thought it was morbid curiosity—a clenching in my stomach—pulling me here. Then people looked sideways at me, said I smelled of the creek. Sometimes, before they blinked and remembered I was a kid, they'd ask advice—as if I understood the troubles adults got into. My own family looked surprised when I showed up for dinner.

And the whole time, this house dragged me towards it.

I started sleepwalking. Every time, I woke closer to the water. Everything I did to stop myself, I'd undo in my sleep. I went to the church—but it was the wrong sort of church. I asked the police. I left Bellworth. Someone always brought me back, and more and more they left me at the *entry* to the street. Such a steep climb, when there was that green fall to the Drowned House.

And my parents kept forgetting I was there.

I was certain someone knew how to help. Someone who'd lived here longer, longest, or who'd at least believe me. But Charlie wouldn't talk to me—Cora and Ida said they didn't want me to upset him. And I was losing my grip by then—I'd set out to climb up to the window of his sleep-out, and end up in a tree at the creek's edge.

I got away, hitchhiking, until I fell asleep in the cab of a truck. When I woke up, the driver had brought me home. But my house was empty. My family had packed up and moved away, and I was alone, except for the Eisings peering from behind their blinds. They didn't answer their door. I went to the Wrens—I wasn't wanted there. Even the birds on the roof glared at me.

I took one last chance. I couldn't risk going downhill, which meant I had to walk past the primary school. Children hung over the fence shouting hatefully, hurling lunches, sticks, rocks. So many of them. Then they jumped the fence.

When I stopped running, here I was at the house of a

murdered man. Sure as a pebble falling to the bottom of a pond. Fifteen, with only my backpack, a shelter I built of rubbish—I refused to live *in* Bill's house—and the bribes people brought when they came for my help. As if I could change anything about the world.

What did I know? I was a kid, not a witch. I made things up—listened for patterns in their stories, looked for the currents in life and pulled at them. Sometimes I can balance desires against each other—mostly only I get hurt. People don't like having their secrets known.

But, technically, I got out of Bellworth.

⚬

Grace searched for a reply, a question, patterns. Roses blurred her vision. She'd was too far from Volney Street, and fading. Soon birds would fly down, pecking at her flowers, her twigs.

"I've waited awhile to tell that," said Liddy. "I've learned a few things since. Now, who's this?"

She was looking past Grace—the dog, too. Grace turned, creaking.

The girl she'd met under Charlie's house slunk out from the trees, then lifted her chin. "I don't think I should tell you."

Liddy snorted. "So precious?"

"Everyone is a Wren or a Braithe or an Eising, like the streets," said the girl, "but we travelled here, and I think I know why my mother wanted us to leave, why my dad—" She stopped herself with a visible effort. "My name doesn't matter."

"Names only count if people make them," said Liddy, amused. "What will you do with my story, now you've got it?"

"I want to know *everything*," said the girl, in a rush. "I'm as old as you were then, almost. I can learn. Teach me! There's nothing in the library and all I have are stories and—"

"You already know more than is helpful," said Liddy. "You have a family, a future. Take them and leave."

"You can't make me!" said the girl. "And my mother died, which you'd know if you'd read my note, and maybe you couldn't have brought Mum back, but you let *her* take the things I left out. It was my *mum's* dress! And Dad's always working so we can afford to move, and I don't want to go. It's my home! And there's a ghost dog and I made that thing Mr Wren brought to you, part of it, and look at her—" She pointed to Grace. "I have to understand. I need to *do* something."

"*I* have things to do," said Liddy. "*I* have things to understand. How can I have answers when people only bring me questions?" Standing, she shook the dirt out of her skirt; the dog rumbled, sun-striped fur rising. "You're contrary," Liddy added. "I met your mother. She tried to be kind when she should have been angry. Still, she was smarter than you—she wanted to leave." She tipped her chin towards Grace. "Take what's left of this one back. Then go, or you'll never get away."

The Fifth Day

AFTERNOON

WIND CHIMES

A family (says the elder Mr Eising) lived in number 18—loud and careless, with too many children and cars. They were old Bellworth stock, so we would have forgiven them that. But not the wind chimes. They collected them, made them, found them—and won no friends.

Notes were delivered. Letters sent. But without a really local representative, the council only does so much. And once you start noticing chimes, they're impossible to ignore. But at last, the family took our hints and left, with their tyres and car batteries and faded toys.

Peace returned. Vada Tepping bought the house, cheaply, for her sister. A nice woman, but shadows deepened under her eyes. "I hear chimes," she said. "All night, every night, and I can't work out where they are."

She searched the neighbourhood by dark. Finally, she climbed into her own ceiling—scrabbling around breathing in dust and fibres is what got her, in the end. But there, in the heat above the insulation, she found the chimes strung along the peak, a jangling spine. Tubes, weights, and bells, she threw them in the bin with a crash like thunder. They clanged again into the garbage truck next day. That was the end of the chimes at number 18.

But what wind was it that rang through her ceiling every night? And does it blow still, now nobody can hear?

CHAPTER SIXTEEN

Through

Humidity eddied among the trees. Charlie, returning through them, felt observed—judged, but never outright accused. The sensation, like Liddy's gibes, spurred him homeward, and lingered as he climbed Volney Street.

"The police were back," called Mrs Braithe from her driveway, making him jump. "Your sister's spread herself thin. Tidy up whatever mess you've made. We're quiet here, and decent. You keep up your end of it."

She retreated into her yard before he asked what she expected of him. Dread sat heavy in his stomach. He wasn't sure for whom.

Number 21 was empty. There was not even the companionable silence of Grace's sleep. The sofa, the beds, the verandahs were unoccupied. He searched for a note, or a sign the police had taken Grace away.

What would they make of her, when they really looked? No identification, no memories, flowers bruising her face. But they must have seen worse. And if they'd taken her, she wasn't his problem anymore.

The gate shrieked. Charlie loped through the house and leaned over the railing as Grace—her weight on the girl—reached the front step. "You could have *died*," he said. "Where the hell were you?"

"Trying not to," said Grace. The colour in her face was wrong; evening and leaf shadows crawled over it.

The kid, sweating, wrinkled her nose. "*I* wouldn't trust him," she whispered loudly.

"Go home," said Charlie. Number 21, never good for children, was worse now.

"No one's *there*."

"Since when do you want supervision?" said Charlie. "Do homework or something."

"Ignore him," said Grace.

"It's my house!" said Charlie. "Go." He clapped as if she were a cat. The girl slunk out, slammed the gate, and ran.

"She helped me," said Grace.

"Then she's done enough. She's better off not getting mixed up with—" He gestured to himself, the house. "Where did you go?"

"I followed you. She followed us." Grace, at the foot of the steps, rested on the wooden bannister. Her smile caught on too-sharp teeth. "Liddy tried to send her home, too."

Charlie didn't smile back. If the police were driving around, that must mean something. If, one way or the other, they'd discovered Alli, he didn't need to fear finding anything in the creek's currents—after all, Liddy, whose corpse he'd been afraid to find, was alive. Here, high up, and not alone, it was safe for him to do what Liddy had accused him of avoiding doing. To look.

Charlie linked his arm around a verandah post and closed his eyes. Quick as touching a flame, he reached for the creek.

There it was, strong in his mind, stitched-through by darting swift lives, matted by larger decay. He pushed aside remembered panic, took courage from the flaking paint and dry timber under his hand, and reached further, beyond Bellworth.

Too far.

A current, swift and deep, took his thoughts. It swept him out of the suburb, through the mouth of the creek, into the river, and flailing for anything firm, he touched—

Charlie wrenched his eyes open.

He was standing on the verandah, cold and sore and gut-sick. Suburbs away, tangled in mangrove roots, a hands-breadth beneath the surface of the broad brown river, were corpse-shreds. Everything that was Alli—the wry grin, the plans, the opinionated effervescence, the hope of a future—had been rinsed away. Below Charlie's lungs, where a few good times and a futile hope had lodged, he ached.

He'd known Alli. He'd liked Alli. Being a Wren, he hadn't expected loss to hurt. And who could he tell? How could he explain?

Grace had hauled herself up the steps, and was in the doorway.

Charlie hadn't done anything—the voice in his mind was Liddy's, flat and accusatory.

"Where did *you* just go?" asked Grace, worried. Her voice threshed, as if forced through leaves. But she was still alive.

He shook his head clear. Put hope into his tone. "What did Liddy say?"

"That I'm too far gone to save."

She smelled of mud, of paperbark swamps, and—still,

always—of clean old cloth. The same as the blanket he'd carried to Liddy.

What was the point in fighting any of this? He asked, anyway. "Did you believe her?"

⚬

The world was splitting open like a seedpod. The taxi driver's daughter had met the not-a-witch, and been called contrary. She had seen the creek-woman up close, spilling flowers, and been trusted to take her home. For all she knew, every house except her own was built on magic and murders and lies. She had a ghost dog, and questions, and a chance of answering them. And who knew what else there was to discover?

At home, in reply to many messages, she called her father.

"I cannot trust you to stay inside," he said. "Tomorrow, you will go to your aunt, until we have a new house." That meant he really was worried—her aunt hadn't talked to him since her mum died. He sighed, then said what he never had before, to her. "Your mother was right. This is not a good place. These people will either use us or end us, but we do not belong, and it is not safe."

She went outside, and angrily rearranged snail shells. Several were newly cracked, and another had shattered outward, as if a too-large snail had struggled to get in. She considered making shell-shaped traps, to catch whatever had broken these.

"I *do* belong," she grumbled, as she adjusted the boundary. Old Ida had let her work in the shed, and taught her how to make that paper face. Cora said she was welcome any time. Only Mr Wren was rude, and she had been helping his friend!

Serve him right if she stayed. She'd belong here even more than he did.

꧁꧂

Grace's joints were separating, but she wouldn't ask for help. Fragmentary flickers had crowded the return from Liddy's camp. Frayed patchwork things clutched at her; a clasping damp presence had waited at the gate. She didn't want to fall apart in Charlie's hands.

Charlie made tea for himself, lemon and honey for Grace's roughened voice. Sitting in the kitchen, they ran through the little they knew, or were willing to tell each other.

Patterns, Liddy had said. Wrens at the heart of them. And too many missing people who were more-or-less Wrens, or connected to them.

On the key map inside the street directory's cover, Gowburgh River—printed an impossible blue—meandered across a ruled-flat city, and spread up into the dense lace of creeks and drains that fed the river. If Liddy was right, roots like wet white hair were filling them, straining the city's deaths.

Spitting out monsters.

Charlie marked places he knew bodies had been found, sites he suspected others were hidden. "A suspicious thing to know," he admitted, lightly. He marked their names, if he knew them. Grace suggested others she remembered from the scrapbooks.

As Charlie examined the map, Grace studied him. He

was drawing a skeleton of the family tree Grace had un-
earthed, its gaps filled by street names. He must realise
that; and when Bellworth banished Liddy, Charlie hadn't
helped her. But he had seemed surprised to find her. He'd
been *happy*.

"Liddy said I stole my face," said Grace.

He met her gaze. She saw the reflection in his eye of petals unfolding from hers—perhaps it was only steam rising
from the mugs.

Charlie looked back at the directory. "All I see is your
face, now," he said. It sounded false. "I really wish I had recognised you. If we knew how you fit, or what happened—"

"Or what I did," said Grace, levelly. "Charlie, you should
suspect me. Roots mean plants, and I'm full of them."

"Those roots were just decay," he said. "Algae or fungus.
Or a disease in the soil, or toxins, fertiliser, poison from the
scrap place in Greenstone . . ."

"Charlie, the yard's *crowded*. The air's flickering with it."

"Heat—" he said, unconvincingly.

"Let's say Liddy's right and deaths are catching on those
tendrils. The thing is, roots anchor something. Feed it."
She pointed to the plant on the windowsill. In the yellowed
water, the seed had split into segments; its widening leaves
were glossy.

"That's an ordinary plant," he said. "It's not harming
anyone."

Grace groaned. If Charlie refused to doubt her when she
begged him to, when he'd seen twigs growing out of her,
what else didn't he suspect? Or what did he know there was
no need to suspect?

He relented. "Look. Did you feel anything when Liddy
tore out those roots, or burned them?"

She'd known sympathy for the construct, fear for herself. And a tide of muddy grief seeping through the trees.

"Did you?" she countered.

"I felt sick," said Charlie.

***

The taxi driver's daughter sat in her driveway, making a trap from paper and emptied eggshells. Eggs, she reasoned, were shaped to hold life, which seemed useful.

The weather was dense, uneasy, and although she glanced up when she felt watched, she didn't expect to see anyone.

Cora Wren stood in the street. She looked as if the humidity had given her a headache. The fragility made her more beautiful—the almost attainable, depressingly distant beauty of an older girl.

"What are you playing?" asked Cora.

"I'm experimenting," the girl mumbled.

"With?"

Although the girl did not want to say, telling Cora felt inevitable as grass through concrete. It was as if her home *wanted* her to.

"Eggs. Ghosts."

"It looks very clever," said Cora, although it didn't.

"It is! They already got into a sculpture I made. Mr Wren and the—and Grace took it to the witch."

"Did they?" said Cora, pleasantly. Her eyes were shadowed. "I saw it—it was nicely done." The girl blushed fiercely. "Did Ida teach you?"

"Not the part with the ghosts. I worked that out myself." Or would, soon. "Do you know about them?"

"A few stories," said Cora. "I'd frighten Charlie when he

was little—messages phantoms scraped on walls at night; old Wrens under their headstones, grumbling about kids these days."

Cora sounded like the professor in those library books, drily retelling tales with no sense of thrilling truth. "Now," she continued, "I think they resemble cats. Looking for a warm spot to curl up in, and then—" Her hand snatched at the air.

Without meaning to, the girl wondered how the friendly, frightened presence had died.

"I prefer dogs," she said gruffly.

Cora laughed. "Come with me. Your yard is too new, too guarded. But mine is the oldest house in Bellworth." The girl knew perfectly well that it couldn't be true, that the Wrens for all Cora's importance hadn't lived here *that* long—only since Bellworth was called that. Cora gave an arch little smile that said, *We both understand what I mean.*

"I know," said the girl. She was crouched grubbily in a driveway, but not ignorant. "I read about it."

"Then you know if there are ghosts anywhere, that's where they'll be," said Cora. "I'll deal with Charlie and Grace—she wasn't even invited." She reached out. "You can take Ida's art supplies and make as many traps as you want."

The taxi driver's daughter wasn't a *kid*, so she didn't take Cora's hand. She sidled down the driveway and fell into step alongside the older girl. Lady. Cora, though humouring her, was the first person at all willing to talk.

"Miss Wren," she began, and wavered.

"Cora!"

"Cora," the girl echoed, self-consciously. "Do *you* know how to catch ghosts?"

"That's easy," said Cora. She tucked her shining hair

behind her ear and leaned in, conspiratorial. "First, you need a body."

⚜

Charlie, in the backyard for fresh air, inspected the leaning fences—number 21 required work, inside and out. *I could stay,* he thought. He felt empty, as if something vital had been stolen, like birds plundering nectar. Work might fill the hollows of a half-lived life.

He didn't want to think about Alli, or Grace, or the impossibility of escape, but decay was thick in the uneven yard. Graves, he imagined—thicker-crowded than explained by a dog and a pigeon. Other, older Wren pets, perhaps. When he kicked idly at an indentation, something resisted and he stopped. He did not want to know if his heel had struck a slick of fur or just plant fibres.

Fallen mangoes, sugar-and-acid, pitted the earth. From beyond the ferns drifted a stench: monsteras putrefying white-lobed from their spines.

Liddy was right. Charlie had survived, and if all he'd gained was knowledge of how death flowed through the city, that was still something. Perhaps even enough to find what they—Grace—needed to know.

He returned to the stairs as if swimming to shore. In the bathroom, the indifferent light was watery. His reflection, when he ducked to look in the mirror, was gaunt.

The episode on the verandah had been coldly factual—he'd known the corpse, not why Alli ended there. His panic by the creek was pure reaction. If he blundered searching through floodplains, he'd incriminate himself. Charlie wished Liddy knew he'd never stopped meaning to leave. But to get answers, he'd have to go the other way.

Charlie gripped the sides of the green sink, closed his eyes, and followed the threads of his senses: lives dissolving. But every adjustment of the dry house, each scrape on the roof, pulled him back.

He was in his own home. Grace was nearby. Charlie was as safe as he would ever be. He ran the bath and, knowing it was foolish, climbed in still dressed, in case he panicked, or drowned.

Water cascaded cool over his hair, his face, and he pushed thought away. The past had happened as it happened; there was no changing it. The bath filled around him. It was not long enough for him, not deep enough for this purpose. He folded his knees up, heels on the rim, and sank into the thunder. Dirt lifted from his hands; along his arms air was trapped, silver.

He felt his way through wider channels. Upstream first, until a barrier obstructed his attention, jangling. The brashness was Liddy's; the territory beyond was hers. He remembered the chimes in her camp, ringing without a breeze, and wondered if she could tell he was there. Then he turned like a swimmer, downstream into Gowburgh, seeking a pattern that webbed the city.

He found it. Tenuous and viscous, it curdled in the creeks, clustered thickening through Bellworth. A net, snarled and beaded with clotted lesser dependencies, gathering and brightening towards Volney Street . . . Charlie sank deeper. Decay brushed past, furred and fluttering.

Charlie, too used to dream-deaths, did not at first notice more than liquid pressing against his nose, his mouth—as if the breath he held could save it. Fingers sharper than splinters scraped his scratched palms, dug like tines into the old scar on his chest.

Mortality overlaid him, a terror not his became his own desperation, blood roared in his ears. Darkness flashed, grave earth rose around, and all his own memories (of a knife in his fist, faces he'd known, the smell of the creek, birds, daylight) were forced through him, out of his chest, and he fought but a hand held him down, tightening on his throat—

WATER TANK

Time was (says Edith), every house in Gowburgh had its own rain tank. Experts decided mosquitoes bred in them, so the city council sent men street to street. They put pickaxes through the iron, and drained them out through backyards and ditches and gullies.

But it wasn't just water. A few crimes nobody asked to have solved were uncovered in the process. And afterwards, people found things in their empty tanks.

Often it was misplaced objects: needles or keys, lost rings, old coins, bird skeletons washed down from gutters—found matted in silt, but until then suspended in weightless dark. The library had a display, alongside the bones someone claimed they found under an old bougainvillea. There was a whole jar of teeth, among other things—hanks of hair, a little cloth bag of leaves well-steeped.

And occasionally, there were objects that couldn't have got into a tank on their own by any imagining, or which shouldn't have gone unnoticed once they did get in.

This was a long time ago. The metal went for scrap, or rusted away before the dams went dry. There's a fashion for tanks again—fibreglass and plastic—and the superstitions have had years to settle. But although the water comes out clear and free, I don't like the thought of one standing silent by my house, or of what might be in it, floating patiently.

CHAPTER SEVENTEEN

Gathering

Number 21 smelled ancient. It was high and shadowy, and old furniture hulked in corners. The taxi driver's daughter lingered awkwardly in the doorway of Cora's bedroom. It was old-fashioned, which reminded her the older girl was, after all, an adult.

Cora beckoned. "Can you climb? I'm not dressed for it."

The girl had to step from a chair to the desk—Cora swept away a handful of exercise books and loose pages (letters, the girl guessed, because some were typed, and the handwriting all different, unreadable cursive and some almost legible). She clambered up onto the bookcase. There was enough room to stand on top of the swaying shelves.

She'd never been afraid of heights before.

"Push aside that hatch," said Cora, far below. The square of thin wood went up into the ceiling. *Spiders*, thought the girl. Hundreds of tiny touches on her face, her neck. She started to scream, then realised it was shrunken flowers. Jacaranda confetti.

Cora laughed. "Nothing worse?" she asked. "Things crawl around up there, sometimes." The girl held the edge of the opening and reached inside. Her fingertips brushed cardboard: a shoebox covered in floral paper. She handed it down and followed, unsteadily.

Cora sat on the bed and opened the treasury. "Aunt Ida didn't approve," she explained.

It held exercise books, fat with curly-lettered notes. They were stuffed with loose paper, some browning and sweet-scented, in old-fashioned handwriting.

"Before my mother died, she'd tell me tales," said Cora. "Most were made-up, warnings or frights. Others . . . My aunt wouldn't explain things to children. So the stories I remembered were a way into knowing about my family, my world."

The girl understood exactly. She wanted to run away with the books, the narrow-folded correspondence, and read herself into the foundations of Bellworth.

"My interests grew," said Cora. "But these will be useful." She tossed across a glittery notebook, which fell open to a page of diagrams: clumsy sketches of animals and birds, and slightly better ones that looked copied. The taxi driver's daughter felt a welcome superiority: young Cora had been bad at drawing.

"Take anything you want from the shed, or under the house," said Cora.

The girl carried books and cardboard, cloth and wire into the backyard. The weight of Mr Wren's disapproval was lighter there, and finally she could make something real. First, she'd build a proper body for the kindly ghost to follow her home.

The clouds towered, glowing white like soapsuds at the top, blue as jeans at the bottom, and she was drunk with knowledge.

⚜

Grace, curled on the parlour sofa, did not sleep. Twice to-day she had risked unravelling. Three times, counting the presence that dissolved into her, under the house. A poor substitute for life, it had changed her again—she sensed thinner draughts; she saw transparent fragments of dead things. She was further from human.

Past Wrens hung above her, smug—they'd left no clues to their crimes. Charlie was calmly ignorant. Liddy offered no hope. And Grace's eyes, although keener, had tired, and her limbs were softening. Charlie would say she should rest and eat, but the little she'd consumed rotted in her chest, feeding the selfish growth in her centre.

Charlie was right. He didn't fight for anything—she couldn't imagine him sustaining enough viciousness to de-liberately commit whatever cruelties had happened here. Yet, however halfhearted, he was alive.

Grace rested her uneven cheek against mangy velour, and waited for whatever-it-was that held her together here to take over.

A tap ran, distant. The floors creaked faintly—Charlie moving elsewhere in the house. The parlour door did not open. Subtly but distinctly, the air pressure changed.

Grace was no longer alone.

Nauseated by airy distortions, revolted by flickers of dis-carded memory, she twisted into the blanket, face against the cushion. She did not breathe, in case a lost thing hissed through the puncture in her ribs.

But this arrival was too solid. It dragged at her atten-tion, pushed against her eardrums, plucked weakly at the blanket, flooded her senses with the dank foaming slime of waterweeds. And a thought grazed hers—*know me.* This wasn't a scavenger, nosing for whatever sweetness it thought the living held. It was the echo of a personality desperate for the means to see, and be seen, and speak.

Grace refused to pity it, or lend her eyes and voice to something so careless as to lose its own. Not even—especially not—if she knew it, or it her. And while it touched, and brushed, and circled, she stayed still as death.

At last, it faded, and was gone.

Grace pulled herself free of the blanket, determined to follow. She did not trust herself alone with the thing, but with Charlie she could hold it, force an explanation.

The taste of earth rose over the parlour's dust and the air, filtered through the glass of door and windows, turned grey green. A crease in it, like a path in long grass, led to the wall by the fireplace. A second door, Grace realised with a chill. How often had she been watched when she was alone?

The unlit space beyond danced with specks. They sparked in the corners of her eyes, evaporated against the roof of her mouth with a glitter of under-floor and hot tin, a coiled smokiness slow as the growth of a tree. Grace covered her face with her arm, and pushed open the next door.

There were no secrets—just the hallway through the house, and the sound of splashing grown louder. Not the contained noise of a basin, but an unceasing cascade.

"Charlie?" said Grace.

At the bathroom, hand on the octagonal doorknob, she looked down. Water lipped the aluminium threshold.

Grace flung the door open.

Her first reaction was resentment. *She* was the one who was meant to be in trouble. Then the compacted futilities of the cloud of tiny deaths through which she had passed, her stifled will to live, and the spark of fury she'd tended against the Wrens drove her forward. She ran, skidding on the flooded linoleum.

Charlie was sunken, unmoving. Clear, green-tinted currents roiled around him, fish-swift and muscular and never quite cohering.

Grace plunged her arms in, tearing Charlie loose, ripping him up through the thrashing ghost. It rushed back into the splitting skin on her arms, clawed at her grasp, but Grace held on.

"Let him go!" she spat. "You've died once. I can end you again!"

⚬

Charlie sprawled shivering on the bathroom floor, retching as much from shock as from what he'd swallowed. Grace had dragged him bodily over the tub's edge and let him fall, hard. But he was awake, and the bruises were his own, and he was alive.

He clung to the certainty of linoleum beneath him, and the garden below it, and Bellworth around. His ribs hurt. Spilled water ran shallow around his shoulders, and the bath still rang, vast and metallic.

"They used to say," said Cora, far above and too steady, "that people who can't be drowned were born to be hanged."

He blinked up at her. The sequence was familiar: sinking, the broken mirror of the surface, Cora's face, late and blurred. She stepped around him, heels splashing in water flecked with dirt and pond scum, turned off the taps, and drew the plug up by its chain.

Charlie, humiliated, tried to spring to his feet, and made it to hands and knees. Behind his closed eyes spun the afterimage of a glowing web.

Cora threw a towel over his hair and ruffled it. "Get dressed. We'll clean up in here."

He levered himself to his feet, and saw Grace huddled on the floor, miserably waterlogged. He'd caught at her shoulder, he remembered. His fingers had pressed wet cloth through gaps like basketwork.

"Grace—" he said.

"Go." Cora pushed him. "I'll deal with this."

⁓◦⊙◦⁓

Grace, face against the floor, felt *ravening*, all red-rimmed eyes and growing teeth. Then she took in Cora's green shoes, splashed dark. Above them, a crisp pink-and-yellow dress; higher still, smooth hair gleaming in the glass-rippled light.

"Clearly I interrupted something," said Cora, looking down, steely and amused. "I can't imagine what."

Grace was once more human, and unutterably shabby.

"Charlie isn't good with water," added Cora. "Or with a lot of things. Did he lash out?" She eyed Grace's torn and bandaged hand. Her concern was cold.

Grace tugged her wet sleeve down. Some of the damage was from Charlie. He *had* fought, eventually. And for a moment, Grace had been invincible.

Now, bruises trickled inky across her skin. The edge of the bathtub had dented her softening bones. She should have eaten the other ghost. But it had dissolved like sugar in Grace's grasp, and she hoped it had washed far away.

She considered letting her roses drink up the overspill, put down roots of their own.

"I wasn't planning to come back today," continued Cora, wiping the cabinet fastidiously. Her locked room, unlike the rest of the house, had been dustless, and Grace caught an impression of the sort of place Cora must live, soulless and gleaming. "But I heard the police saw you and thought there was . . ." She paused tactfully. ". . . cause for concern."

Grace forced herself to stand, and Cora leaned against the sink, hands loosely clasped. Ready to talk, ignorant of what Grace saw: her own face, or what had been a face, reflected in the mirror behind the halo of Cora's hair.

As long as Cora didn't realise anything was wrong, Grace could pretend the same.

"Charlie didn't attack me," said Grace. She wasn't sure how to explain to his sister, tidy and reassuring, that something had gone after *him*.

"Grace," Cora said, gentle but distinct. "This is my house, my suburb, my career. My brother. If anything— even Charlie—threatens those, I have to know."

"He wasn't drowning himself!" exclaimed Grace.

"Poor Charlie." Cora held out her hands and Grace automatically extended her most-injured arm for Cora to examine. Limp brown leaves edged out from beneath the knot. Cora ran her cool fingers pensively over the twisted cloth, up the fraying inside of Grace's wrist. "It's not a crime to be unlucky in friendships. And I'll always save him."

Cora's eyes, so like Charlie's, studied her, and Grace, hurt and startled, realised Cora *did* see the truth—Grace's stolen face sloughing back to her first featureless mask, rose-stained. Cora's interest was simply academic.

Cora must have channelled all her emotions into her

career and her brother, with none to spare for reacting to monstrous sights. What if Charlie, equally, was unfazed by things conscience or distaste should have prevented him doing?

Charlie, it struck Grace, was easy to mistrust when he wasn't in the room; he became so quickly a stranger, and she doubted him all over again. Grace wasn't alone in that, of course, but Liddy—who had known him well, once— had been disdainful, not afraid.

Grace wanted to owe Charlie nothing; she had struck at him, she'd insulted his family. Yet he'd let her in and stitched her together. He'd laughed on the bicycle and saved the plant on the windowsill. That wasn't nothing. *I keep deciding to trust him*, Grace told herself. *I have to remember that.*

Cora's shell-coloured nails dented Grace's skin and Grace pulled away. Hating the petulance in her own voice, she said, "It was ghosts."

Cora, faced with Grace, should not have laughed at the concept. She did. "Oh, they make a good story, but they keep to themselves. That's the point."

"They aren't, though," said Grace, rubbing her wrist, pressing it into shape. "They, or something transparent, are getting into things. Like mice into pantries, or hands into puppets. Like—like backed-up drains. I've started seeing them."

"Really?" Cora's merriment faded. She looked worn down. "Why now, do you think?"

"I don't know." Grace was tired, too. "It's not my house."

"No," said Cora. Her expressive eyes deepened. "Have you considered," she asked, delicately, "that something might have stirred them up?"

"Yes!" said Grace. "But who? Not Charlie. I don't know

how—I don't *want* them." She refused to admit she herself was a symptom, let alone a cause. "Liddy doesn't either."

"Liddy?" echoed Cora. Her surprise, though mild, was so genuine that Grace realised it hadn't been before, when Grace mentioned ghosts. "Is she still there? I'd assumed she died." Cora sat a moment, amused by something far away.

Then she agreed, "No, not Lydia."

Lydia. Grace tried to remember what Cora had implied, when they first met—that a Lydia had disappeared, that it had perhaps been Charlie's fault. But Cora nodded to the window over the backyard. Deepening sky and overgrown foliage mingled in its dimpled glass. "There's a little girl outside, playing at ghosts—or with them. She was making herself at home here before Ida died. Taking an interest. Even, or especially, if she hasn't the least idea what she's meddling with, has anyone spoken to her?"

⁂

Charlie, in the sleep-out, had run out of clean clothes, but at least he had dry ones. He changed unsteadily, then towelled water out of his ears, his hair. His sense of the creek, the net, the yard, was evaporating.

"I told you to get rid of her," said his sister. She leaned wearily in the entry from the sewing room, her head against the doorframe, tilted back to look up at him. The police, Charlie remembered. Whatever had brought them back would be yet another worry for her—

"Cora," he began, not sure how to phrase the question.

"You trust too easily," said his sister. "And you choose people who are volatile. Look at Alli, storming off."

"It wasn't like—"

"You don't know who Grace is, or what she's capable of."

"She rescued me!"

"Eventually," said his sister. "No, listen to me. That person, Grace—if that's her name—is too comfortable here. Too comfortable with *you*, although I told her about everything. She's persuasive, yes, but you're suggestible. Look how guilty you act whenever you're questioned. The police would have happily arrested you this morning, if they'd had any grounds at all." She hesitated, then added, "They seem to have had difficulty reaching the house to check on you, before that. As if someone didn't want them here."

"But—" Charlie heard the complaint in his voice. He cleared his throat, spoke definitely. "I haven't done anything."

"I know!" said Cora. Exasperation made her look young—a schoolgirl, almost a stranger. Even in nightmares, Cora as she'd become, calm and capable, had overwritten the Cora who'd saved him. Charlie was heartened; memories changed once could be changed again.

Cora was still talking. "I accept your universal innocence, Charlie. But most women I know—most men!—won't trust an unknown man easily. Especially not one so unnecessarily tall, who is known to the police."

Charlie put that together and took offence. "I should be suspicious of Grace *because* she's not afraid of me?"

"No! I'm saying you nearly drowned today, people keep vanishing"—she did believe him—"and even careful people are more likely to traipse off with a woman." She raised her eyebrows as if to say, *Look how I found you.*

"If you're saying Grace is a murderer . . ." He had no plausible evidence she wasn't. Since he came back to Volney Street—since Grace arrived—reality had become a kaleidoscope. He kept hoping he'd understand the pattern, but he wouldn't be able to defend his reasoning, once Cora analysed it.

"Charlie," Cora said, firmly kind. "There's going to be trouble again, over Alli."

He scuffed the floorboards with a bare heel.

"Will you trust me?" she asked.

"I always have, haven't I?"

He met Cora's gaze and knew he was ungrateful. He wanted to offer something—an apology, a reliance. "Ida never had pets except Dennis, did she?" he asked. "Why does the yard feel full of them?"

"Since I don't live here," said Cora tartly, "that's a question for your guest." She looked askance at his daybed. "Where does she sleep?"

⁂

In the parlour, Cora pointedly shook out Grace's tumbled blankets and folded them, and brushed a few dead leaves off the sofa. She checked behind the canvas-work pillows, drew the toe of her shoe under the sofa, returning only dust. Then she knelt and felt underneath the seat cushions. One, two—and three. She glanced up at Charlie, then withdrew her hand.

In it rested a charm, a tiny aeroplane. Charlie had seen it before, tucked into Alli's wallet. He'd never brought Alli here.

Cora lifted the cushion. In the sag of the dusty velour clustered a few shreds of fabric, an earring Charlie didn't recognise, and a heavy silver ring with the face of the moon along its edge.

"That's Micah's," said Cora softly.

"No," said Charlie.

Cora, still kneeling on the floor, glared up. Most of the dead—the missing—had been her friends, too.

"What is Grace doing here?" she demanded. "What is she *hiding* here, in a big old house no one visits, with a yard no one can see into, so near the creek? What will they dredge up, if they search?"

An image of ghosts crawling from the soft earth, worms rising to the promise of rain.

"Grace rescued me," Charlie repeated. He was losing his certainty.

"Did she?" He wasn't sure if she was irritated more for or at him. "Or were you getting close to guessing? Or maybe you were *convenient*? You were lucky I arrived."

"I always am!" snapped Charlie.

Cora stood. Her face was drawn and pale, and he stepped back because she looked too small, with all the weight of both their lives on her shoulders. The unlit room was growing dark.

"You were lucky," she repeated. "Where is Grace?"

MOON

When my wife's grandmother (says old Mr Eising) was a girl on the other side of the world, no one dared leave a dish of water uncovered to the night, for the mirrored moon was a door. As for what could enter through it? A few said it had long spidery legs, or was an impossibly handsome man. Others claimed it was both at once.

My wife's grandmother said her grandmother was either lazy or enterprising. She put a basin in her window one full moon, and caught herself a husband. But she was cleverer than kind. He begged to leave, promised to return with pearls and white gold. She wouldn't tell him the way. She emptied bowls at evening, threw pebbles at reflections in the stream.

But running water holds its own dangers. Green and mossy beings, annoyed, reached dripping hands to her husband. They told him that in stagnant pools, or when water slid in a pure flow over a stone, the moon slipped aside as if something waited behind it.

The next full moon, she woke to a splash, and found on the threshold a pail of water, rippling as if a stone had fallen in. She never saw her husband again.

My wife's grandmother said it was just a tale—after all, there are many ways to find and lose a spouse. But she warned us not to throw stones into running water, for who knows what bad luck that might bring?

CHAPTER EIGHTEEN

Rising

Ghosts—called or welcomed or stirred up like silt, ghosts trapped and building up like sediment—were rising fast in the storm-light. Liddy might have noticed, but the taxi driver's daughter was busy with her framework.

She'd constructed a small body (just the size for a dense-bodied dog) of string-knotted twigs, trimmed to length with a rusted box cutter from the shed. Torn strips of pillowcases thickened and hinged the limbs. She'd hung a heart inside it, from Cora's room—a bright bangle, since the dog (existing at the Wrens' house) must have belonged to and recognised Wrens, and also because the bangle was like one her mother had owned. And when she succeeded at not only befriending a ghost but giving it a shape, Cora would be astonished, and ask her name, and treat her like a grown-up.

Presences—unfelt yet unsettling—washed through the grass, piling over each other in flickering hunger. They fluttered the notebook pages past flowers drawn for some purpose other than beauty, and animals splayed and labelled which were not, the girl suspected uncomfortably, *living* animals, and shook free a torn scrap—part of a letter (*I have seen before and I know. Please please* please *consider*) written in urgent nearly forgotten handwriting, not Cora's. That was an investigation for later. Right now she had to concentrate on ghosts, and not on a memory of her mother's hand shaping cramped ballpoint sentences, while a shining bangle knocked against the table.

Her ghost, so brave in the shed, was outnumbered now. It pressed suddenly close and cold, draining warmth from her side. The box cutter slipped—swift and efficient along her finger. For a moment, the cut was dry and pale. Then blood welled along it.

And things with mouths, and mouthless things, leapt to press against her hand. Fragments crowded through the blood, clung and climbed invisibly up to her neck, her mouth, her eyes. They wanted, perhaps, no more than to taste a breath, or borrow one; to shout the one word remaining in the emptiness of themselves.

But she was a kid, and there were too many.

***

Billowing spirits distorted the girl like a specimen in glass and Grace stumbled down the steps, towed forward by air rushing into the vacuum of the basket body. She tore the framework from the girl's hands and smashed it to the ground. Ghosts spun like birds, but Grace did not stop until it was sticks and rags. She had staggered upright and away, shaken by her own violence, before she realised the girl on the grass hadn't protested.

The child was choking. Glassy phantoms bubbled pink-foamed around her mouth and thrashed like leeches on the bloody hand that scrabbled at Grace's bare foot, smearing the pages of an open notebook.

Grace watched.

The girl needed air. But if Grace took breath to give her, or drew contamination *out* of the girl, she herself would inhale those hungry fragments. It was hard enough defending herself as it was.

She felt no urgency. Her rage over the attack on Charlie was spent. This girl was a fool. Grace owed her nothing except a small gratitude for the bandage on her hand, and the shamefaced moment they'd shared, contemplating Cora Wren.

"*Grace!*" Charlie's voice was distant.

The spirits were regathering. Grace, not breathing, bent into the narrowing ripples and flicked to the first page of the notebook. She had not seen it before in her searches, but inside, in large confident writing, was written *C. M. Wren.*

This, then, was not entirely the girl's fault.

Resigned, Grace loosened the damp fabric around her own wrist, leaving the faded pattern printed on her skin. She caught the child's hand and wrapped cloth around the cut finger.

Then she seized the girl's jaw, forced back her head, and began fishing fragments of ghosts out of her throat.

⚭

Cora leaned along the kitchen counter to reach the knife block. She passed one to Charlie. "In case."

The bone handle sat too comfortably in his hand. He was off balance, half drowned again; shaken loose from what he'd started to grasp. "In case *what*?"

He reached the kitchen door and saw. The girl was suffocating, and Grace? Grace stood over her, and did nothing.

"Go!" Cora said, and pushed. "Stop her, or this time it *will* be your fault!"

Out the door, down the stairs, still trying to understand. All his questions coming loose: why anyone would keep killing Wrens, friends, neighbours. Surely they were guilty of as little as Charlie. *Cora* had barely managed local fame—too anchored by him, when she'd been destined for more.

He sprinted over the grass. Thunder rumbled; wind buffeted him. Grace held down the struggling girl.

His nose and lungs were raw, and the dark garden was lengthening. Charlie lost patience. "No!" he shouted, as he had when the birds chased Grace.

Time and distance snapped into place.

Stop her, Cora had said. And he had a knife. But Grace was seated, her bandage on the girl's hand, and the girl was coughing limply into the grass, and at his feet a book glimmered out of a memory—Cora yelling at him when he found her diaries.

Grace raised an arm, and Charlie pulled her to her feet. Something popped and tore in her shoulder.

"They're thinning," she said. "The ghosts. Did you do something—"

He glanced back. Cora, elegant, had descended the stairs. "Charlie," Grace hissed. "She *knew*—"

Cora picked her way over the grass.

Charlie rarely needed to think quickly, and he had little reliable information: dream-habits, crimes of which he'd been suspected, what he understood of Grace. He linked his arm around her throat, knife against her shoulder.

Grace lashed out, but she was weak. "I didn't!" she

choked. "It was Cora's book. And she knew, about Liddy. You're not—"

"I know!" whispered Charlie, tightening his grip. Louder, for Cora's benefit, he added. "I saw! The—the *trophies* under your sofa. The dead animals."

"What animals—" Grace dug her fingers, blunt now, into his arm. At their feet, the girl stared up in terror. Charlie, glaring, willed her to lie still.

"And the drownings?" he said. "They weren't *my* memories. They weren't memories at all."

Grace kicked.

"I never killed anyone," he said. Any clearer, and his sister would hear. "You don't have to trust me, but *listen*. Either way, we both know you're already dead." He dropped his voice. "And she has to see."

Cora had reached them. "What are you waiting for?" she asked, and gestured to the girl, very still. "Look what she's done."

Charlie was holding the knife where he'd felt the gaps between Grace's vines, where he hoped there was least risk of harm. Then Cora folded her hands around his and drove the blade home.

Charlie jerked back, towing Grace with him, and stumbled over the girl. His knife ripped up through the vines, snagging and tearing. They fell together, and Cora followed, pinning Grace to the earth.

Charlie struggled free, and grabbed his sister's arms.

"She attacked you," said Cora. "She's killed before."

Her hands, still on the knife, tangled the layers of Grace's shirts into the wound—if *wound* was the right word for what was no longer bone and muscle, and perhaps never had been. But Grace didn't move, and Charlie had to act as if it didn't matter—as if he were relieved.

Cora let him drag her hands away, tendrils snapping on the withdrawing knife. She didn't even look surprised—merely mildly dissatisfied. The emotionless Wrens. Standing, she became more interested in the white scratches left on her own skin by splintered twigs.

"No blood," she murmured.

"What have you done?" said Charlie.

Cora's smile flickered. "Your hands were first on the knife." She bent and pressed under Grace's jaw, hard enough to bruise. Hard enough to tear. If the thorns pricked her, she gave no sign. She did the same to the girl, who kept her eyes shut.

"Not dead," said Cora. "But her pulse is slowing. Poor thing. Ida seemed fond of her."

"Let's go," said Charlie, catching her elbow. "Give me your phone. I'll call an ambulance." Sounding shaken was easy—the violence had been too familiar: his hand on a knife, a death, and the fleeting sense of being *alive*.

"And say what?" said Cora, invigorated by the struggle. "You invited a murderer here? This was self-defence? That your house—"

"Ours," said Charlie.

"—mine, if you prefer, is filled with evidence linking you to Alli? To Micah? And how many others?"

"The kid's alive!"

"Not for long." Cora put out the toe of one of her water-stained shoes and prodded the girl's arm. It rolled nervelessly, curled fingers brushing a bracelet half trodden into the grass. *Graveyard tag*, thought Charlie.

"You'll go," Cora decided. "We'll bury them first. No

one's going to search *my* house, and even if they did, the rain will have washed any other evidence away. Anyway, you've been wanting to leave."

He wondered how far she'd let him go, and what would happen here. *Keep up your end of it*, Mrs Braithe had said, as if he'd left a responsibility unfulfilled—he'd never been told what. Cora always said—casually, as people did—that he didn't know what they had. He'd assumed she'd meant he was ungrateful. But perhaps it meant she *did* know.

Cora, brows drawn in mild concern, reached to touch his cheek. "Can you manage digging a hole?" She nodded towards the shed. "You've left the shovel out again."

"You put it back," Charlie realised, another piece dropping into place. "The day you met Grace. What were you doing?"

"Tidying up." She gestured to Grace and the girl. "Put these in the shed, in case someone comes looking. I'll stop that—you made it too easy for people to get in the gate."

He remembered the magpies attacking Grace. "What are you going to do?"

"Supervise," said his sister. Her grin was brittle, and he still couldn't fear her—she was, eternally, Cora. She added, with a touch of superiority, "After all, *I* didn't kill anyone."

<hr />

The knife had cut too deeply for Grace's vines to mend; if something vital had been severed, she did not have strength to care. A spark of green had flared in the blade's retreat; a memory below memory assured her it meant *life*. But not for her. And scavenging ghosts were gathering.

Grace fled inward. Far away, her unravelling body was

lifted, and a remote voice said, "Remember, you're both dead."

It was very distant.

Time returned with a revulsion of sweetness. She was, somehow, still alone in herself, except for the fumes in her skull.

She scrambled outward into her limbs, spat out something small and hard, and groaned for want of words.

"Shh," said a voice she knew. The girl. "We're playing dead. I tried to move your head and my fingers went right into your skull and I almost *did* die. I only had mints to give you, I'm sorry, but they're strong."

Charlie's arm, Cora's fingertips had crushed Grace's throat. Her destroyed shoulder was bare, except for a wad of cloth forced in there, pushed down into the cavity of her chest. She plucked its folds, and stirred up the soap-and-cotton taste of old clean sheets, reminiscent of her roses before they'd begun to wilt. It cut fresh through a flatness of oily dirt, the tang of iron.

She was on the floor of the shed, in grey twilight. The girl had plundered the bag of bed linen Charlie dragged in for the last corpse.

"It's another pillowcase," said the girl. "This one matches your tattoos." Grace twisted towards the crumpled dressing, but the girl leaned to peer into her face. Grace *had* seen her before, mirrored. *Stealing reflections from puddles in the reeds.* Who'd said that?

"If you're alive, or if you can stand, I can get us out. We'll have to sneak."

"You leave," Grace rasped. "Charlie promised not to kill me." A day—a lifetime—ago, and meaningless. Charlie had guessed she wasn't alive to begin with.

The fabric in her shoulder was patterned with blue roses. They caught against the dying twigs of her own.

"Getting buried might kill you," said the girl. "Mr Wren will do whatever Cora says, and she—" Indignation stiffened her voice. "She sent me outside to be eaten by ghosts! I thought she didn't believe, but now I think she *made* some of them. Especially the dog, and I like him more than I ever liked her."

And there was Grace's answer. The vines weren't an infection, but an outgrowth. *Let them have grown from some good memory,* she wished pointlessly. Outside a shovel struck singing into soil, and it was too easy to picture a body buried in a flower-printed sheet: decaying, eroding except for one insoluble shard that woke tangled in roots. And then, clinging to a flotsam of other spirits (murdered and lost, human and animal), returning to the source of its shroud, only to be murdered again. That was where everything she was came from: the overlaid recollections of Wren faces, the sliding glimpses of a city across years, the fright and senses she had stolen from smaller ghosts she had engulfed—rat, snake, cat. And the knotwork of blue roses binding them together.

But she didn't want to be that—a mash, dried and cracking, of bits no one wanted, too foolish to either stay dead or remember how they got that way.

Grace searched for her old sustaining rage. It did not respond.

The girl's hand—slippery with fear, gritty with dirt and blood—found Grace's papery palm, and held on. The cold loop of the bangle knocked against Grace's knuckles.

If saving the girl from the Wrens was the purpose driving Grace to survive, her duty was done, and she could disintegrate in peace.

Grace didn't believe that. But she was too weak to leave, and as a parting gift, she willed a memory—the green spark of life that had followed Charlie's knife—into the hand pulling at hers.

"Come on," the girl said. "I'll fix you."

There wouldn't be time.

Rain had begun, like pebbles on the roof. The taxi driver's daughter whispered to the dog—in case it was near—to stay on guard. Then she let herself out of the shed, alone.

The clouds overhead were low and woolly, and she was sick with fear of the living as she hadn't been of the dead. When Cora's cool fingers searched for her pulse, the girl had *felt* her heart slowing. She was still cold around her chest, except for a little desperate flame.

From what she'd overheard, Cora would be watching the street. The girl's leg ached from when Mr Wren and Grace had fallen on her. She imagined limping to the gate under cover of the ferns, but her mind skidded queasily away, as if the front garden was an oily blank.

And in the huge backyard, pitted and spirit-ridden, Mr Wren's shovel was cutting the ground.

Rain splattered on grass. The side fences were high, and braced from the other side; she saw it as clearly as if she'd seeped through them herself, and grimaced. This was an aftertaste of knowledge from the ghosts she'd choked on. She wanted to scrape the roiling awareness off her tongue, to spit out the bitterness of crowding trees, the sour garden tilting down to the ditch between yards, the muddy flavour of that drain steepening from school and graveyard to the creek . . .

The ditch!

The clouds were heavy and bruised. Elsewhere, uphill, it would be raining properly, yellow mist sinking over Gowburgh's hills, steam rising like phantoms from hot roads. The worst weather might miss Bellworth, but rain went where it pleased, and now it rolled towards them.

Acid fright—not all her own—burned her throat. She held her breath and slid into dusk. Rain, loud on the flattening canopies (mango, umbrella, mulberry), hid the scuffle of her shoes. Mr Wren was facing the other way.

A hopping dash took her into the deeper trees. Scraping her shins on branches, she slithered through twigs and under netting, out of the sparking gloom and along the shadowy gully. The bangle snagged on twigs, but she tore it free and forged on, her sneakers full of water.

Where the row of houses ended, the drain passed under a culvert. By the time she stumbled into it, ragged breaths trebled by concrete, the trickle was up to her ankles, and she blundered into the rusted web of a sunken bicycle. Out the other side, the night changed loyalties, broadened, pebbled with warm rain. Bamboo chattered between whispering trees, and mud sucked at her feet.

She glanced once at the misting of light uphill, but knew exactly where to go. She pulled herself up a ladder of exposed roots and onto the path to the Drowned House.

She burned with life. The rain and the rising creek explained everything: the sound of footsteps, fleeting anxious touches, a wet stump flashing a bone-white face. And she was outraged. Cora Wren had sent her to play with fire, and had killed a dog, and Mr Wren had left Grace—whom she'd thought he *liked*—on the floor of the shed, bleeding blue petals.

Where clouded evening broke through, water glinted like steel. Liddy knew she wouldn't do what she was told, and that meant what Liddy had really said was to be angry, to find answers; she'd as good as told her to come back, with a name or without one.

Chains and mats of leaves were joining in the flow; soon it would cover the crossing to Liddy's camp. The girl ran. Even limping, even in darkness, it was better than crying.

As she went over the matted fence out of Bellworth, vines and weeds snatched at her, but the path beyond was *expectant*, and besides, she was too furious to stop.

The Fifth Day

EVENING

ORTON

The trouble with night-driving (says one of the tradies) is wildlife. That's what got Orton. He shared with us in Greenstone, and lived for his motorbike. He repaired it in the lounge room, screamed down the highway, and parked in the garden. The old ladies next door hated him.

You don't see many animals in Bellworth, but over the highway and further out, there's all kinds. Water dragons, kangaroos sprawled around the prison, feral deer, and some it's harder to place. Drive in the dark past the training range, and there'll be eyes shining reddish white through the fences, higher than they should be.

Orton talked about those, a lot. I ignored him, until one night I caught a lift in his ute. On the roundabout, Orton hit the brakes—two huge white dogs were in the road, eating. They looked up, heads high as the window. And then, calm as you like, they strolled by.

"They're following me," Orton said.

Soon after, he crashed his bike. Said he swerved for a deer; burned his leg because he hadn't wanted to kick the motorcycle off, and risk damaging it. He got done for drink-driving.

"I lied," Orton told me when he got discharged. Crutches and all, he was leaving town. "It was those dogs. They stood judging me, and I was scared to move in case they made up their minds."

CHAPTER NINETEEN

Not Noticing

Charlie had stepped into the deepening grave, the better to dig. Twice, something crumbled chalkily under his shovel. He didn't want to know what—the Wrens had lived here too long.

Charlie had always assumed his sister knew best; now he suspected she simply knew more. With his record of not noticing, surely she'd accept he hadn't seen the girl limping to safety.

Sweat trickled down his back; rain spattered between the leaves. His scratched hands stung. When Grace slipped away, too, he'd stop, and when Cora heard—well, what harm had he done? Grace's story would be implausible. Normality would return, with no responsibilities, so long as he pretended ignorance of what never bothered him before.

The smell of mud was thick enough that he could have sculpted the suburb—not the unfamiliar landscape banked and rebellious beneath, but his Bellworth, webbed and anchored in place. And in it, small as a snail shell, a miniature Charlie, digging a hole in a garden that coiled like intestines between and behind the fences, too large for the space between the houses.

He was ankle-deep in slurry; death, smelling of macadamias and rotten fruit, rose around him.

"That's enough," said Cora, above. She was barefoot, with Aunt Ida's old raincoat over her flowered dress.

Charlie climbed onto the grass and followed his sister, hoping Grace had escaped—he'd learned how silently she moved. Hope stirred the leaves.

But Grace was motionless, a pile of clothes on the shed floor.

"Charlie," said Cora, sweetly. "The child appears to have gone."

"Good," said Charlie. He tried to feel more than weariness: pity for Grace, or relief for the girl. Horror.

Cora gripped his arm. Although the bloom of excitement had gone from her cheeks (*She doesn't* bring *brightness, she* thrives *on it,* thought Charlie), she was strong. "No, it isn't *good.* You think we've been here this long and there aren't people jealous of us? Waiting for us to trip up? *Prying?*" Her voice shook with frustration. "I hadn't planned for that tonight, but if they interfere, after all my work, all the responsibilities I've taken on—"

She broke off, and reset her rain-whitened face. "Bring her," she said, and tramped away, hands plunged into the raincoat's pockets.

Do it yourself, Charlie wanted to say. But this was Grace, and he bent to lift what remained. She seized the front of his shirt.

Charlie leapt back, and Grace—hands twisted in his collar—followed him up. "The roses are from here," she rasped.

He didn't know how she was alive, but he was grateful, and gladder than Grace was.

She jerked her chin to the crumpled fabric packed into her shoulder. "Look." Charlie recognised it this time: the print of blue roses. He'd cleared out Ida's linen cupboards himself, he remembered tracing the patterns on that pillow when he'd been sick—

Grace pulled her eroding face closer to his, and hissed, "A body was wrapped and rotted in that cloth, and some part of it is me, and if you bury me alive, Charlie Wren, I swear I will never stop haunting you."

Rain ran into his eyes. "I'll think of something," he promised. Grace's clothes, heavy with rain, weighed more than she did, but even so he wouldn't be able to run fast half-carrying her. And in truth, the world outside the garden no longer seemed real.

"What you'll think of, Charlie Wren," said Cora, from the graveside, "is what the police would say if they'd seen what we found." She faced them, her face small inside the hood. "I don't need to keep you out of trouble anymore—*I* can survive a scandal. Anyway, the prison's over the highway—I'll barely miss you."

"But you *know*—" began Charlie.

"I'm the only one who does!" said his sister. "Be reasonable. Remember what you owe to me—to everyone. People rely on us to do what's right, to tell them the right thing to do. The gifts on the steps aren't from sheer neighbourliness. Good God, did you *let* the girl go?"

"You said she was nearly dead," replied Charlie.

"What's nearly dead is *that*," said Cora, at Grace. "If we had time, I'd take her apart to find out what keeps her upright. You don't owe her anything. She had trophies from Alli and Micah, and who knows who else—you saw the bangle she dropped when she went for the girl. And she tried to kill you." Cora pointed to the grave's deeper darkness. "Push her in."

"No," said Charlie, propping Grace up. He'd always gone along with Cora before, and he felt her stare at him. He had to play for time.

"A ghost attacked me, Cora. Grace saved my life. I—I was pulling at the threads of something. I *touched* it. It sounds ridiculous, but the things going on are bigger than us. Bigger than Grace. Maybe it's one of your—our— enemies, or a natural phenomenon—"

"It's not natural," said a grim voice.

Cora's gaze glinted towards the house. Charlie staggered around with Grace. The kitchen windows, scattering highlights across wet leaves, silhouetted Liddy. Her hair was flat and her skirt hung heavy, clinging against her gum boots.

"Lydia Damson," said Cora, flatly.

Liddy went on. "It's dead, but growing slimy roots anyway. *I'd* ask what horrible body is sending them down. Or maybe I'm alone in thinking it's bad work, choking things that just wanted to die quietly, fishing them back up until they have no choice but to pretend to be alive."

"Go away, Lydia!" snapped Cora. "Vanish back into your creek! You aren't wanted."

"I noticed *that*," said Liddy, with distaste. "The front yard's greasy-feeling. But you weren't paying attention—a little welcome was waiting."

Cora wrinkled her nose. "Charlie, of course."

"No. He invited me too, though. And isn't this his house as much as yours?"

"Charlie," said Cora. "Get rid of her."

"Liddy," begged Charlie, knowing Cora would think he was being ineffectually obedient. "It isn't safe."

Did the kid fetch you? he wanted to ask, and *Did you get her clear of this?* But a shadow wavered, furtive, in the kitchen window, and he doubted it.

Liddy squelched towards them. "A little bird told me life was going cheap in Volney Street and I thought, *Oh, again.*"

Cora spoke through gritted teeth. "It's not your business."

"I wanted to catch up with old friends," said Liddy. "It's been years, and I wondered if they'd changed. At all." She switched on a heavy torch and shone it into Cora's face.

Cora didn't blink. "You have a shovel *right there*, Charlie," she said.

She meant for him to hit Liddy. That realisation struck hard. He intended to resist, but Grace, as stilt-uncertain as the thing he'd killed in the garden, moved first. She crooked her arm around his neck.

"And I have Charlie," she said.

Liddy made an impatient noise. "This was never about him."

Cora laughed. "Of course not. Let him go, Grace."

Grace's hold tightened. She wasn't strong enough to strangle him, but Charlie clawed at her wrist, as if panicking. Together—Grace's feet snagging in the grass, Charlie keeping them both upright—they stumbled from the grave, away from Cora, towards the bottom of the yard.

⁊⊙⊱

Grace saw contempt flare in Cora's torch-bleached face.

"I'm not worried about Charlie," she said, and turned to Liddy.

"Get to the drain—" whispered Charlie, then slipped. They slithered together down the last of the slope, into swift shallows, grass-clotted. Sprawled there, Grace heard Liddy shout, "She's lying!"

Grace had only malice left to burn, and she owed Charlie a fright. "Trust me," she gasped. "But hold your breath."

Liddy's rain-strobed torch swung past Cora and picked them out in the tunnel of bauhinia leaves. Grace fastened her hand over Charlie's mouth and nose, and pushed his head down into mud.

With her remaining strength, she held him under. It would be so easy to let the water in: retribution for what he hadn't done, for what he hadn't known. And how could she trust him to play dead for her sake? Cora was his *sister*.

"Stop it!" ordered Cora. Grace, wanting to obey, leaned harder on Charlie.

"He's mine!" shouted Cora. "I *spared* him!"

She lunged downhill, but Liddy pelted after her, flung the torch down, and seized the tail and hood of Cora's raincoat. Cora spun and Liddy stayed behind—towing her away, going through her pockets.

"You're bluffing!" Cora sounded ready to cry. "You'd never let her hurt him!"

"I might," Liddy growled. She released Cora, recovered the torch, and held up a knife. The edge caught the light like a thread of rain. "Do I need to choose one of you?"

Charlie started to struggle properly, but Grace—even fading—held him. He'd trusted too long.

POPPIES

My great-grandfather (says a teacher from Eising Street) learned, at war, to cut himself for the dead. He was in the trenches where men died so thickly they could not drain away, but bubbled in the mud and crowded the nights. Dank and cold, he incised them into his skin. First, he carved a line for his brother. Then for those who fought beside him, even some officers he served under. Nurses who died in a bombed hospital train. Men he killed. Too many scars, ridging his arms like graves.

He never spoke about the war. My grandmother did not find his diaries until she was grown-up, and he didn't record who taught him this. But as she read, she remembered that when he came home, and until she forgot he had ever been any other way, she would glance at her father, and see other eyes look back.

CHAPTER TWENTY

The True Story

The taxi driver's daughter was sweaty with fear and running, grimed with the slippery unwelcome of the front garden, the overflow vomited from the severed downpipes, the dust of the Wren's house. Liddy had sent her up the stairs and inside alone, to gather supplies, and now the girl was almost glad to be in the backyard again, leaves spilling clean water down her neck. Her vision still sparked with embers of infesting memories, but as she crept along the fence, one ghost flowed like warm fog around her shins. Together, they set out tin cups of milk and sugar from the kitchen, bloodied with the cut she'd reopened on her hand.

At the end of the garden, Cora glowed in Liddy's torchlight. And the girl, pausing, thought, *We outnumber her. We could knock her down, wrap* her *in an old blanket and shut her in the shed.*

Cora's voice was calm, and peace rose from the earth, settled steady as an arm across the girl's shoulders: *Be patient, everything will be clear.*

She wanted that like the ghosts wanted life.

"Let him go," said Cora. She dragged fingers through her wet hair and smoothed her dress. "*Please*," she added, elaborately polite. "Grace—or whatever you are."

"Don't you know?" Grace taunted. She'd hoped Cora did. "How many people have you wrapped in old sheets and buried, or sunk in the creek—"

"It's a misunderstanding," said Cora with dignity, then added, "For pity's sake, let him breathe! It's necessary for some. And he isn't smart enough to have done any of this—I swear, Charlie Wren, if you don't stand up for yourself, I'll rip off your skin and wear it to fight *for* you!"

Grace let Charlie force himself out of the mud, and kept hold while he coughed out leaves and water, and swore.

"Hush," said Grace.

❦

Charlie was ready to scramble, retching, into the undergrowth and not stop until he was out of Bellworth. But Grace's grip, now, supported her more than it restrained him; he stayed, and watched his sister warily.

Cora, shining hair plastered along her face, dress mudheavy, was regal. "*First*," she said, to Liddy and Grace, "no one needs Charlie. I've put him to use, and he is my brother. But I'm the one who's necessary."

"Oh, please explain," said Liddy.

Cora, long-suffering, sighed. "Charlie's never been practical. He hasn't done anything wrong. He hasn't done anything at all."

"I want to know what *you've* done," said Liddy. Charlie didn't.

"I'm telling you!" snapped Cora. "We'd have been sent

away, or worse, after Mum died. I kept Dad's people from wanting us. *I* made us stay. Not in spite of her stories, *because* of them. Bellworth is ours. Generations of Wrens are buried here—"

"Anyone can be buried," said Liddy. "Plenty of families have stayed, or struggled—"

"Or killed," Grace rasped by Charlie's ear.

Cora nodded graciously. "Yes, whether to keep a place or take one—everyone does that, too. But not like us. I worked it out. There was evidence, rumours. You'd be surprised what people leave in drawers and books, what neighbours will tell a schoolgirl researching an assignment. And once you have a few secrets, it's easy to gather more."

"What secrets?" said Charlie.

"See?" said his sister. "Charlie wasn't curious—he wouldn't have noticed if we'd lost it all. Aunt Ida was smug, wasting the potential, the *power* of us on—what? Playing with paper, making the neighbours look after her, keeping trees flowering out of season—and not letting anyone else have a turn. But I pieced together what it meant to be important, and a Wren, and how."

"How what?" demanded Charlie.

A ripple of water distorted Cora's disapproval. She shook it off, dismissing Charlie's tone, just as she ignored Liddy's knife, the grave.

"Such a clever trick, once I reasoned it out—simple, deniable. Graveyards fill; that's what they're for. *Died quick, died cold, moved slow, was bold.* Remember? No one wonders at a few unfortunate deaths in a family. Think about Mum! She came here to die—you never thought to wonder why she got sick? Ida was greedy; she had Mum's jewellery before she was cold."

Charlie had been young, but he'd never heard anything suspicious. "People die, Cora!"

"Not like Wrens," she said. "Not in Gowburgh." Beneath Cora's compelling voice ran a soured, childish bitterness. "The snobs who think they run this city? One good storm, and they'll run to higher ground. They won't leave a trace. Wrens put down roots. We reach through our dead and pull the earth back up into ourselves, whether it—or anyone else!—wants us to or not." Old anger shook her voice. "All that potential—and Ida wasn't using it. So I made my own arrangements."

Liddy had spoken of the great cost of tiny powers. But Cora was here, and herself; whoever had paid, Charlie doubted it was Cora. "Do you mean *sacrifice*?" he asked.

"Murder," said Liddy, flatly.

"Nothing that melodramatic," said Cora. "Or mundane." A grin crept into her voice. "I just needed to kill my brother."

She looked pleased at their silence. Then Liddy exclaimed, "I knew it!"

"You didn't know anything!" snapped Cora. "It was a Wren tradition—and if it was the only way, I'd have to act before Charlie did it to me."

"I wouldn't—" began Charlie. He sat up straighter. Grace's arm, in his grip, was a shifting wickerwork of bones. "And besides, I'm alive."

"You'd have done worse," said his sister. "If you'd noticed the truth—and it was right there, in the games, the house, the graveyard—you'd have been too timid to claim it. You'd have burned it, run off, wasted away in another city. No more Wrens. But I wasn't going to let Aunt Ida keep everything of ours for herself."

"I knew something was wrong," repeated Liddy.

"You blundered in," Cora retorted. "You, and that interfering old man. Bill *Volney*—as if his name was as good as Wren. Listening at the edges, stealing scraps, keeping secrets."

"Keeping the boundary!" exclaimed Liddy.

Charlie, abruptly as falling, understood: The confused impressions of that day in the creek made sense, once he stopped fitting them to the wrong story. Cora—sixteen, unwanted, struggling for a foothold—had held him under.

"He wanted to stop you," he realised.

"I saw something," said Liddy, with childish relief. "I shouted and he ran to help, and no one believed me."

"Annoying, but timely," said Cora. "Because I realised Wrens still die—the entire suburb was proof of that! What was the point of losing my brother to gain a little control, if some fool might take it into their head to kill me as easily? Ida would certainly want to get rid of me, if she knew. But I'd done my research—Charlie was only my first *person*. I knew what it might be possible to claw away from the edge of existence, fold into a cooling body. And I'd have other uses for Charlie."

She had turned the knife, Charlie understood now. She'd pointed it at herself instead of him. And holding his hands still clasped around it, she'd driven it into her own chest.

Memories came into focus, untangled. The guilt of deaths not his. The reflection of his own face, separated from Cora's by water. And the creek drawn through both of them, like thread through beads, so he'd never shake either it or his sister.

Grace gave no sign of what she thought. He crooked his fingers over her arm, under his chin. Frail as rotten wood, but still there.

"Because Charlie didn't know how to hook through life

into the earth," said Cora, "how to siphon the sweetness, I did it for both of us. I *died*. Then I climbed right back up us both. I was in my body before the old man dragged us out. When he was shaking Charlie and telling him *drop it*, I was already there."

"He thought it was my knife," realised Charlie.

Cora laughed. "He meant for you to drop *Bellworth*. And you agreed—you'd have accepted anyway. You didn't want it like I did. So Charlie—*poor* Charlie—murdered his sister, and I did nothing wrong at all."

Gleaming with pride under the rain-rattled leaves, she said simply, "I won."

The rain quieted. Reflected lights shimmered as the leaves stirred.

This version felt finally true. It dragged liability with it, and obligation—and something like courage.

"Nothing *wrong*?" repeated Liddy.

"She's dead." Grace's whisper startled Charlie. "She's a ghost in a frame, but she's lived for years and years and I've only had three days."

Liddy still shone the torch into Cora's face. "And Bill Volney?"

Cora shrugged. "Why ask? You both benefitted."

"*Benefitted?*" exclaimed Charlie.

"Lydia got a purpose. And you—oh, Charlie, you've always had me to catch you. You've got away with so much, so *little*, for so long."

"I haven't done anything," said Charlie.

"Exactly," said Cora.

Bowls of rain-thinned milk and blood shone like dim moons, and ghosts blurred, pulsing, above. *If they won't stay dead, let's give them something to be busy about,* Liddy had said. The taxi driver's daughter suspected that had just been to keep *her* busy. She crouched in the ferns, clutching the short kitchen knife she'd used to reinjure her hand, and wondered if she could go as far as Miss Wren had. Kill to belong. Die to own.

She envied and resented Cora equally. *Do something,* she told herself. *Run in and kick her, and maybe everyone else will finally move.* Her legs didn't obey.

Cora, toes clenched in the wet grass, stood as formally as if giving a classroom speech. Even the shadows on her face didn't make her look old.

If she's dead, the girl realised, *she's still a teenager! She hasn't grown up in all those years. She's exactly what she wanted to be then, and will never be anything else.* That wasn't what *she* wanted at all.

And watching Cora tire, she relaxed.

*

Liddy swung the torch towards Charlie. He eased Grace's arm away, and propped her against a cushion of matted twigs, her feet in the water. Then he followed the beam uphill until Cora shifted, and Liddy again shone it on her. Cora smiled.

"What happened to Bill Volney?" Liddy repeated.

"That's right," said Cora. "Your family locked you in, the night he died—they always did think they were better than us. They left easily, though—shallow roots."

"And Bill?" prompted Liddy, grimly. Liddy, who had been left behind.

Cora spread her hands. "Bellworth was so newly mine—all I had to do was grant permission. *Boys and girls, come out to play.* Nobody trusted the old man—and kids enjoy rough games." Her face, torchlit, brightened with wonder. "I wish you could understand that first breathing in, by choice and not need. The power of it. *My* power. Ida could control a child, prompt a neighbour, persuade a gallery owner. I held the reins of the suburb."

"Except Liddy," said Charlie, approaching cautiously. He'd felt Cora push him to strike Liddy, and resisted. Perhaps he'd learned to hold his own, perhaps it was easier once someone knew what she could do. And she looked tired.

Cora scoffed. "Who believed her? How far did she get? You should thank me, Lydia. The old man filled a purpose in the world, after all. He must have left a socket like a knocked-out tooth. You'd have finished badly, without that hole to slip into."

"And what have you done since?" asked Charlie. It was too large a question: What of other claims to the land, after or alongside the Wrens, or before them? What about the neighbours, however much they understood? And Liddy, once his friend, and Grace, whatever she had been? And the lost, and the missing?

"I saved Bellworth," said Cora. "Without me it would be another Greenstone! Factories and scrapyards and prisons. The worst weather goes around us, the floods don't reach our house. Our secrets stay buried."

"Your secrets?" said Grace. Charlie glanced back.

Opaque water frothed the deepening gully. He felt it gathering uphill, beyond the graveyard; downstream, it pulled silky and violent under the culvert, into the rising channel. Grace, who looked like creek-wrack washed up among the bauhinias, grasped an overhanging branch and, somehow, stood.

"What happened to them?" she asked. "The ones who got in your way?"

"No one did," said Cora. "I managed everything so elegantly. I'd sidestepped Ida—left her as much as she gave us. And although she could never work out quite what had happened, she felt it. It ate at her until the end."

"Did you kill her?" said Charlie.

"She suspected I knew she killed Mum," said Cora. "It was enough that she thought I was poisoning her the same way." She added haughtily, "*I* had refined the technique."

"She got out," said Charlie. It meant there was hope.

"I wore her down," said Cora. "That hospital was hardly an escape."

"But others died," said Charlie. Underfoot were hollows, small and large, that had been bodies. Rot washed in the channels, presences shivered the undergrowth.

"And weren't you happier pretending not to know?"

"Did you murder them?" shouted Charlie.

Cora, closing her eyes briefly as if pained, didn't ask whom he meant. "They were *us*. Survival is justifiable. And no one can commit a crime once they're dead."

Charlie forced himself to match her cool tone. "Survival? It wasn't self-defence, if nobody guessed how clever you were."

"For fertiliser," said Liddy, audibly revolted. "She's been growing through them, putting down roots."

"And the animals?" said Charlie, not sure if he meant *why them* or *why not them instead of us, instead of Alli.*

"Food, at a guess," said Liddy. Charlie remembered—unwillingly—the pigeon he'd found half gnawed, as if something had been interrupted at a meal; the posters of missing pets. "But Cora's ambitious. She's roamed, tying Gowburgh to herself. Making a mess, and running out of Wrens."

Ghost-nets, like the tendrils Liddy had burned, stuttered in the edges of Charlie's vision. Cora, torch-whitened, makeup washed away, looked half his age.

"All my friends," he began. Corpses dissolving into Gowburgh.

"Poor Charlie," said Cora. "I'm sorry. Mine too, you know. They were so barely related to us, by the end, that I had to make them mean something to a Wren to be useful. They went with me gladly. They wanted something brilliant, and since you couldn't be that, I was."

Behind Charlie, Grace—Grace, who was falling apart, who had arrived unshapen and accusatory as an unmarked grave—asked, "What about me?"

Charlie, almost close enough to reach out to his sister, hesitated. He didn't want Grace to have another name, another self than the one he'd watched her mould.

"What am I now?" Grace demanded. "Who was I?"

"Honestly," said Cora, wearily. "I don't care."

Too late, the taxi driver's daughter noticed a current strengthening in the yard. Not water rippling through the grass, and not the ghosts—they were preoccupied with easier food. This was a flowing will, a desire to be somewhere, and before the girl caught herself, she was in the open.

Liddy, feet braced as if against an outrunning tide, seized the girl's arm. "Run," she growled.

"That worked so well for you," said Cora. "And I'm stronger now."

Liddy's grip slipped and slid to the girl's wrist. "I won't let you—"

"Dear Lydia," said Cora charmingly. "For once, understand this isn't about you."

The girl twisted her hand to grasp Liddy's, their muddied fingers slimy with blood.

"If people say something isn't about you, it is," whispered Liddy, ferocious. "*Fight.*"

"Oh, Lydia," said Cora. "I didn't say it wasn't about her."

The girl tried to hold her ground. But she was younger than Liddy had been, and unlike Liddy, she'd admired the Wrens. The cold threads that had tied her to Cora when she played dead tugged her off balance. Her hand jerked from Liddy's and, windmilling her arms, she ran into Cora's grasp.

⁂

Charlie, who had not expected either the girl or her headlong rush, lunged too late.

"There," said Cora comfortably. She took a knife from the girl and settled it against her hostage's neck. "Now go away, Lydia."

"Cora, let her go!" said Charlie.

"Charlie," his sister reproached. "Grace can't help you,

and Liddy never did. I've protected you, constantly." She brightened. "I'm delighted you can finally appreciate it. All that power is anchored through you. That sense of the waterways is a party trick—I'll give you more power, enough to be thoroughly comfortable."

The knife scratched the girl's jaw. Her eyes widened, but she kept her mouth shut.

"What do you want, Charlie?" asked his sister. "To fight what's already happened, or accept what you've always enjoyed? I've succeeded at everything I've ever done! And you can live well here, too. If anyone bothers you, we'll deal with them. And the neighbours—they pretend ignorance, but they've lived with us for generations."

"Not everyone!" said the girl. "I know! My father—"

Cora clamped her hand over the girl's mouth. "Your choice, Charlie."

This is still my sister, Charlie told himself. Yet if the dead could have a claim on the living, why should Cora have priority? She'd taken Liddy's future, and killed Alli, and the others—all those nightmares he'd woken from guilt-ridden and refreshed. She'd tried to kill Grace, and the girl. She'd spared him, and for fourteen years he'd been cramped into half a life, so that Cora could have room to grow.

If he took it back . . . But there was nowhere solid to stand in his own mind. Nothing he could grasp to pull himself clear of Cora.

"Charlie," said Grace. "Ghosts."

He wasn't imagining them. Traceries shifted, glinting in the weeds. These wore no shells of paper and bark. Luminous as jellyfish, they crawled through the ferns, their transparent forms coalesced around fanned-coral branches of white roots, like afterimages of lightning.

They had come from hollows below the garden, pits in the dirt, mudbanks, strategic burials longer ago. Too many wrongs to right. *Breathe.* Alli's advice. *Make a list of what needs to be done.* The deaths, the power, all traced to a single point. *Wren*, the first thing Grace had said. *No good ending.* Liddy's words.

There was a simpler way.

"Liddy," he said. "You have a knife—" And Charlie didn't know how to ask an old friend to kill him, and quickly.

Cora, thinking he meant for Liddy to attack her, laughed. "You won't risk the girl."

"No," said Liddy. "Not her."

Ghosts circled, darting towards the girl and trembling away from Cora. Entertained, she said, "Look after yourselves. They can't hurt *me*."

"Can't they?" said Grace.

⁕

Using a broken branch, Grace had pushed herself uphill into the yard. Ghosts—floating fronds, sketches of once-living forms—phosphoresced around her.

The shred of strength she'd saved against a vanishing hope of living, she spent now. "You owed them a proper death, at least," she said, one clouding eye fixed on Cora. She didn't think the other was an eye anymore—the air *ruffled* it, and Charlie, Liddy, the girl blurred into night. "Not this: inhuman, crushed into the wrong shapes, decaying."

"To be human is to decay!" said Cora. "Look at the garden. Look at Lydia. Charlie, send them away."

And Grace guessed the answer: Cora didn't know how

to quiet the dead. And while Cora—clasping an unwilling hostage—still needed Charlie, she had been disappointed of two lives today. What would happen when only Charlie was left to sustain her?

And Charlie, ever less like Cora, was still Cora's brother.

"Go," he said, over his shoulder.

The push was tentative, but Grace stumbled. "Don't!" she said. "You idiot!"

"Get away," said Charlie, as if he believed she could.

Grace lost her temper.

She'd held it in check so long that letting go shook her. "Fine!" she snapped, and dropped her walking stick. She ripped the wadded cloth, with its printed woven roses, out of her shoulder, dragged the bandage from her neck, extended her fraying arms and let her head drop back.

"Don't be dramatic," said Cora. "Whatever you're doing—"

For days, after defining her own edges and taking a name, Grace had fought off other ghosts. Now, she drew a single, long breath, and compressed what remained of *herself* (angers and terrors, desires and memories of how many corpses?) deep within the cage of her chest.

And the ghosts, a white-water of light, followed.

Her flaking layers of skin rippled. Her body was loud with splintered panic. She didn't have what they wanted. But for a few moments, they would fill out the collapsing spaces in her frame.

"Stay where you are," said Cora.

Grace—or something in her—lurched forward. Shards of fear, of hunger lanced through her body.

"I will kill this girl," said Cora.

Grace veered behind her. Cora attempted to spin around. "Where are you *going*?" The girl had made herself a deadweight, and something in Grace knew to feint. First a wounded drifting towards the house, then a spur-winged dart back at Cora. She plunged her hand over Cora's shoulder, and punched through thin skin and rotten bones, into her chest.

Through breastbone and ribs, Grace's fingers, shredding and fleshless, splintered into Charlie's sister, closed, and ripped out . . . not a heart. A snarl of fibres, peaty and earthen, trailing frail tendrils and a taste of death old and sweet as grass before rain.

The other spirits—her temporary passengers—blustered past Grace. She was a sinking ship and Cora a lifeboat. An outrush of mangled recollections clambered from her impossible body and poured into that lovely container, brightening it from within.

⁂

Charlie tore the girl out of Cora's arms, flung her at Liddy, and caught his sister as she fell. She gasped at nothing, frantically pressing closed the ragged hole in her chest. Glowing filaments spilled between her fingers.

"Charlie, *get them off me! Get them away!*"

"I don't know how!" She'd been about to murder a kid. She had been dead for years. But she was Cora. He owed her this—not to let go yet. "You never told me."

"You didn't *ask!*" whispered Cora, folding to the ground, gaunt as their mother, her face falling into itself like the paper head. "That child worked out more—you don't deserve what you have. If one of us has to end up a ghost, Charlie Wren, it will *never* be me."

She slashed up—fingers and teeth and the short sharp blade in her hand—and tore out his throat.

NIGHT DRIVING

You see things at night (agrees a quiet neighbour). Not haunt-ings. The rumble of a lost tram route, a vanishing passenger? Those happen everywhere, any time. But streetlights turn the world's pale belly up: houses towed away with their ghosts; vast mining machines crawling inland. And passengers with the echo of a second voice and a reflection that moves too soon.

A friend picked up a fare, early-early on a factory road where spotlights make potholes into canyons. She was not in hi-vis or heels or travel-crumpled, did not drunk-laugh or burn with nerves. She was normal, flower-bright; her reflection as smooth as if it practised, her words exactly from her own mouth.

My friend can chat, but the more his passenger answered, the unhappier he was—the way when someone jokes, expecting you to laugh, and it is too late to tell them the joke is about some-one like you. He was afraid if she said more about her day, he wouldn't enjoy it at all. So whenever she paused, he asked other things—"The house fire, you heard . . . ?" "The murder, do they say . . . ?" "Was the animal caught . . . ?"—until they arrived.

Then my friend did two things he never had before. He did not charge for that long drive. And he left without making sure she reached her door.

But still her stories run around his head, scratching to get out.

CHAPTER TWENTY-ONE

And So It Goes

Charlie didn't hear the girl finally scream, or Liddy swearing. He didn't see Liddy hold Cora back as she burned herself out, thrashing free of a body worn too long past dying. He did not register Grace frantically failing to pin his throat together against his blood.

He did notice, mildly curious, that this was a new death, thundering and hot. Easier than he'd expected. The yard softened into silt. No silver air lifted from his open mouth. Bellworth ran upward into darkness.

Obligations he hadn't asked for drifted away. Responsibilities to his neighbours. To Liddy. To Grace. To the little tree on the windowsill, which he'd never plant out. He was fleetingly sorry.

⚜

The taxi driver's daughter stopped screaming when she hit the ground. For a moment, she lay petrified where Liddy dropped her, staring into the open grave. Wet, torn fabric hung from the side; it stank of rot, and the edge was slumping.

She scrambled away and to her feet, dragging the shovel, and swung it up to strike.

She was too late. The ghosts were withering, dimming as Cora faded, vanishing into the night.

"No!" she said, dropping the shovel and reaching after them. "Come back!" Although none of them quite matched a dog, she didn't care. Whatever that cringing comfort was, she couldn't lose it. All it had wanted was to stay.

"Tell me its name!" she wailed. But no Wren could answer.

"Try Dennis," said Liddy, gripping Cora's wrists with large, dirty hands. The other woman, almost properly dead, hardly struggled.

It was easier to panic about a long-dead dog than to watch.

"*Dennis!*" the girl shouted, trying not to sob. Once she started feeling anything, she'd feel everything. She knelt in the mud and clapped. "Come here!"

And there it was, thinning, frightened, and trusting. *He* is *a dog*, she reassured herself. The lung-shaped veins of guttering light looked like too large a creature crouched in too small a space. But those were the webs Cora Wren had spun, that the ghosts stuck to. It didn't mean anything about Dennis.

"Stay," she ordered, firmly. "You don't need her. You've got me."

Liddy, who was peering into Cora's face, said, "Careful. And go home. If anyone asks you—"

"I'll lie," said the taxi driver's daughter. She stood, wiped a filthy arm across her face, winced, and swallowed. "What about you? What about the police? And—" She lifted her chin so she couldn't see Mr Wren dying. His blood was black in the night. She wanted to offer something. "I took a first-aid class."

"I doubt it covered this," said Liddy drily, and crossed Cora's arms over her broken chest and the ruined bodice of the flowered dress. "As for Charlie, there wasn't much to begin with, and now Cora's gone . . . He's better out of it."

Water dribbled slowly out of Mr Wren's neck, flecked with leaves and twitched by ghost-fragments. And Grace was a twist of vines and grey bamboo, blue petals trodden into mud.

The girl wanted to fall down and shriek until someone carried her to bed. The fury that had fuelled her was all gone. She took a shallow breath, and another. Too fast.

"It won't be a problem," said Liddy. "If anyone finds out the truth, who'll be alive to mind?"

If the girl started thinking, she'd care too much. She had Dennis, and tonight that was enough. Tomorrow, she would work out what to feel, and ask.

"Close the gate," said Liddy.

There wasn't enough of Grace for the ghosts to scramble back into. The net that trapped them, and to which they had clung, had crumbled when Cora's heart did. Grace held only the residue of desires not to become nothing.

A curlew sobbed in the quiet after rain. Fences sagged creaking in the dark, sodden branches groaned. Something marvellous and murderous had been torn from the world; Bellworth subsided slightly to fill it.

"People will look." A voice, elsewhere. "No reason they should *find*. The ones who'll understand? No sense giving them ideas." Liddy bent into Grace's segmenting sight. "You're going, too."

What had briefly gathered to be Grace was flaking into

the mud. And Charlie was gone. *Take his corpse,* said the last flicker of her will to live. *Become a hollow hungry thing, like Cora.* At least she would *be.*

She waited for Liddy to kick her apart, and stop that future.

"Well," said Liddy, her voice hard and shaken. She stood. "This has not been a pleasure. I'm off—there'll be water damage to deal with, and I have a job to do. But at least people can get on with dying, now."

This was not how things were meant to go. "No—" Grace thought, or said. The sound might have been trees settling.

"Tidy up when you're done," said Liddy. "Leave me out of it."

She took her torch with her. Night, starred by distant windows, washed over what was ceasing to be anyone at all.

⚬

People always left; this time it was Charlie's turn. But as he sank into unfathomable depths, he realised someone had followed him down.

She'd shed her face, compressed her remaining shards into a self like a handful of nails. He'd have known her anywhere. She seized him by the ragged edges of his wound.

"Charlie!" A fist slammed on a stopped heart.

There never had been enough of him to save, but he couldn't tell Grace it was pointless. He had no air, no mouth, no lungs.

And she was splintering away.

"I trusted you! You swore not to kill me!"

On his life. He remembered. A promise carelessly given, their first day. But he'd kept it. There was no reason for her to shake him, not enough Charlie to blame. Death was meant to be peaceful.

"Charlie! I can't carry us both. I *won't*."

Charlie had been carried long enough. He'd never asked to live.

"You survive this long with her leaning on you, and suddenly you choose not to? I'll become worse than Cora if you don't wake up!"

Mud thickened, welcoming.

"What have you got to lose?"

Peace. But he moved. Kicked weakly, and was drifting up, then rushing, too fast. Out of the silt, into the wet night, the blood, the drowning weight of wet clothes, knowledge ringing like a knife on a stone.

He vomited leaves and flowers. His throat was filled with barbed wire.

"This is worse," he rasped.

There was no one in the yard who could hear.

And yet, he wasn't alone. Mismatched memories, razor-edged, jangled against his skull. Some were missing. Many weren't his. But for once, he knew whose they were.

⚜

The taxi driver's daughter stood for a while with her hand on the scrolled iron gate of number 21. Numb and wretched and hungry, she still wasn't ready to turn her back on this forever.

Finally, she left the gate just wide enough for an animal to slip through and limped down the street.

The chimes in the gardens were silent. The Eisings' sailboat-windmill listed, becalmed. But the night air was cool and easier to breathe. Water shook from the mock-orange, trickled down gutters, whispered in storm drains. Running to the creek.

From her own driveway, she looked at these houses which always weathered the worst storms. At the crest, the graveyard was anchored by bodies. And in the Wren house, one family had squatted for years adjusting Bellworth around itself.

Her father wasn't home yet. There was no one to lie to her for her own good, and tell her everything was fine. It never had been, and wouldn't be—her mother had known that, and even before this, Liddy had said *you already know more than is helpful*. Eyes stinging, the girl pressed those thoughts flat and folded them away for later.

Indoors, she washed off mud and blood, bandaged the cut on her jaw and others she didn't remember getting—twigs, or wire, or reaching claws. She ate without tasting, and went to bed, the bangle hard and real under her pillow, where she'd folded her mother's dress. Proof of *something*. Tomorrow, she promised, she'd learn—whether Liddy wanted to teach her or not. She'd work out how to make her father forget to worry, and stay. She'd make people *want* to know her name. And then she'd make them earn it.

A few minutes later she felt a soft pressure against her feet, as if something had curled on top of the blanket. She smelled, for a moment, a scent not quite that of a dog.

⁂

Pain was as new to Grace as the mosaic of selves was to Charlie. They lay for a while on the grass, breathing: the involuntary breaths of the living, unfamiliar to one as they were unexpected to the other. The darkness was too vivid, their vision complete—blue green with knowledge of what the Wrens had taken, and worn, and kept; refracted with the night vision Grace had stolen from one or other of her ghosts; rustling with the knowledge of not leaving, of not having been left.

Time slowed, sweetened. With the skill of practice, they stitched themselves together.

You came back/you stayed, one or both of them thought. Which? It would never be possible to tell. *We should be horrified/furious/grateful/unsurprised.*

We?/Ourself.

Before dawn, they were able to stand: coltishly unsteady, and laughing. The tangle of matter—dead roses and cloth, jewellery and rot—that had held all that was Grace, that had been Cora, they pushed into the grave and reburied.

And it was easy to let the too-large yard fold on itself, until it filled only an ordinary amount of land. They pushed it beneath notice, and recognised how it felt to do that. Part of them had done it before on the night when, half wakened by headlights, Charlie had willed a patrol car away from the street. But this time they gloried in it, a little.

Old bones remained in the suburb, true; evidence of vanishings drifted in the floodplain. But the creek, tonight, was subsiding quickly, and the dead (not all, never all) flowed out with it. And they were not among them.

At daybreak, someone crawled up the stairs, filthy, bloodied, not yet easy in their skin, exhausted with exhilaration and power and grief, and a hundred emotions they would have leisure to name. They were neither entirely Charlie, nor Grace, nor any of the deaths whose fragments had formed her. They were something new.

Beyond coloured windows, cobwebs burned gold; lorikeets hung shrieking among flowers. The roads were lace-edged with tidal traceries of leaves, the puddles held only sky, and violet morning shadows were empty of watchers. The world was, briefly, as clear as glass.

And the new person in the Wren house was aware that they could walk away—let the house fall, call trees to grow over it, permit the highway to widen. They'd be gone before the yard was dug up. They might not even be missed—already, they felt other bright wonders, shining horrors, unfold from stumps and packing cases, lower themselves out of ceilings and memories where they had lain cramped for decades, or a century, or more, ready to fill the hollows of Bellworth. And along the creek Liddy was walking, followed by her strange brindled dog, and a girl, and an eager rustle in the grass . . .

But there was no urgency. They'd have time to destroy the evidence, the trail of pebbles Cora had left as insurance. To unpick, if they chose, the knots the Wrens had tied, and let the stain of the family fade out of Gowburgh.

They could make time. Hold Volney Street still, for a little, while they worked out what to do with both a life and a will to live it, with their wariness of responsibility and the desire to understand this power. With the cautious overtures of neighbours who guessed a little, or with those who knew.

And surely the Wrens weren't the worst secret in the city. It would certainly be easy not to be the worst Wren.

DANCING JENNY

When I was a very small boy (said frail Mr Braithe), my big sister would put up her hair to go to dances with soldiers at the hall—where the golf range is now, on the floodplain. My mother warned her to be careful. But my sister laughed and said there was nothing to worry about nowadays. I used to sit on the dressing table and hold her hairpins, and one evening, when my mother left the room, I asked my sister what she meant.

She looked at me in the mirror and said, slyly, "There was a girl who was drowned in the creek. But late at night, she creeps up the banks, all muddy and weedy. She walks in her rags barefoot over the road—I know someone who saw her in their headlights—and creeps up to the hall windows to watch the dancing. Sometimes her wet footprints are still outside next morning. But if a man is about to make trouble"—she turned and clapped her hands in my face—"SNAP, she drags him away to the water, and he never does that again."

CHAPTER TWENTY-TWO

Flood Nights

Flood nights are dark, but not silent.

The rising silt pushes aside the bright, busy wonders of Bellworth, for this is one of the nights the creek claims its own. The creek shifts and changes; it slides like fingers through hair, stirring grass and gardens, enveloping house-stumps and floorboards.

Volney Street and its neighbours are cut off, and for a few hours, while the air smells first of rain and then mud and slow vegetable death, ghosts wash back in.

They rise from hot bitumen, arrive on the damp breeze, or carry on eerie lowing from the paddocks beyond the Drowned House. (A young woman emptied its clotted rooms and lives there now. Some claim to have seen her and old Liddy slipping in a canoe from door to door, robbing sunken properties—the truth depends on what it is they are said to steal.) And when the creek retreats, leaving trees plastered grey and rubbish clogging the footpaths, spirits will rustle and rummage in the detritus.

And this evening, the neighbours—Eisings and Braithes and Teppings—have pulled chairs into the street. Even (to do him justice) the Wren they know as Charlie is there, lanky and unremarkable except for the tattoos around his throat and arms. Thorns, and blue roses.

Only the taxi driver, who lives nearest of us to the creek (and has lost, in his way, the most to it), does not join us.

Stories told every flood year are told again—a little more polished, a trifle more entertaining (no one discusses why it is *these* stories they tell). Occasionally, there is the kingfisher-flash of a new tale. After all, not every warning is heeded.

And when they go home, torchlight bobbing from pane to pane, they leave their windows open against the heavy air. Some dream they hear a soft scrabbling at the screen. Others lie awake, listening for the lapping water to bring footsteps to their doors.

Acknowledgments

Honeyeater is dedicated to my sisters Angela and Rebecca, who are very kind, well-adjusted people.

It is also a love letter to streets I've lived in, and "a river with a city problem" (as quoted by Margaret Cook)—the city that lives in the songs of The Go-Betweens and Ball Park Music and many others. To my neighbours there (including but not limited to Chris and Barrie, Scott and Carol, Margaret, Diane, Aaron and Dyanne, Faye and Graham), thank you for so much help and friendship and so many stories during and between floods, including the one that happened while I was editing this book and the one that is probably on the way as I write this. To my housemates over the years (including Becky, Aimee, Rachel, Liz, the Auchenflower girls, and dogs Diesel, Rosie, and Sam, and occasional visitor Lucy), thank you for all you brought to this story and my life.

Everyone who has influenced this story is a lovely normal person. If they read and suspect any echoes in this, I hope they understand (as I have told them!) that when I like something in real life, I show it by making it creepy in fiction.

Ellen Datlow edited the book rigorously and thoughtfully, and also demonstrated a great deal of patience and understanding along the way! Thank you also to Matt Rusin, editor, and all the team at Tor, particularly Claire Eddy and Will Hinton (editorial directors/publishers), Devi Pillai (president/publisher of TPG), Samantha Friedlander (marketing), Cassidy Sattler (publicity), Jim Kapp (production manager), Dakota Griffin (production editor), Greg Collins (designer), Terry McGarry (copy editor), Marcell Rosenblatt (proofreader), and Ed Chapman (cold reader). Thanks also to the team at Picador, including Cate Blake and Claire Craig.

My PhD advisors, Professor Kim Wilkins and Dr Skye Doherty, advised and supported me through several unexpectedly complicated years, and offered inspiration, friendship, and side quests. Thank you also to my examiners Dr Marshall Moore and Dr Tim Jarvis, for their valuable time and thoughts on the novel as well as my broader dissertation, and to the Australian Government for a Research Training Program Scholarship. And to the shut-up-and-work group at UQ—I wouldn't have got to the end without you!

Many friends helped me get *Honeyeater* written. Alex Adsett generously provided space to write and accepted late-night texts of tiny creepy stories. Karissa Chang was the very first reader of the first few chapters and confirmed that there was, in fact, a vibe. Isobelle Carmody, Elizabeth McKewin, Lisa McNally, Alex Adsett, and Jo Anderton (who also proofread the final PhD manuscript) provided feedback on early drafts and, in Liz's case, suffered bravely through having a housemate on book *and* PhD deadlines. And Angela Slatter (as ever) provided thorough and incisive commentary to shape the final version, and much other advice along the way. Thank you also to Shena Wolf, my agent, who joined the story of *Honeyeater* in plenty of time to experience the melodrama of me getting anything done.

To everyone who read the pitch or manuscript and said such lovely things about it and reached out to me directly in the lead-up to publication, thank you. This includes Laird Barron, Ruoxi Chen, Paul Cornell, C. S. E. Cooney, Irene Gallo, Owen King, T. Kingfisher, Elizabeth Knox, Thomas Lloyd, Delia Sherman, Francis Spufford, and Angela Slatter. It helped a lot.

Books are supported in many ways. Darryl Jones's request that I illustrate his (delightful) *Curlews on Vulture Street* gave me a lot of local material and excuses for research. Ali Denman-Mills and Jo Anderton lent parts of their names. Elizabeth-Jane Baldry and Pigwiggen Woods, and Château d'Orquevaux both gave me time and space to edit and experiment on this book (and another), and enchanted company and settings to do it in.

The first glimpse of the world that became *Honeyeater* appeared in my short story "The Splendour Falls," originally published by *Andromeda Spaceways Inflight Magazine*, and released again by Small Beer Press in my short story collection, *Kindling*. And as those who pay attention might notice, *Honeyeater* isn't entirely disconnected from the milieu of *Flyaway* and "Undine Love"—all gratitude associated with *Flyaway* before and after publication applies here, too.

Gowburgh and Bellworth and Volney Street (like their residents) are fictional. But they were influenced heavily by places I know and in which I have lived, most particularly the lands of the Jagera and Turrbal peoples.

Finally, thanks most especially to my parents, Mark and Mary, for their endless support. I was going to read *Honeyeater* to my father when the copyedits came in, but never got the chance. He always let everyone know that he delighted in his girls. I really liked him.

About the Author

KATHLEEN JENNINGS lives in Brisbane, Australia, a subtropical city with certain similarities to Gowburgh.

Her Australian Gothic debut, *Flyaway,* (set in Western Queensland, where she grew up) received a British Fantasy Award (the Sydney J. Bounds Award) and was short-listed for the World Fantasy Award. She is also the author of a short story collection, *Kindling,* and a poetry collection, *Travelogues: Vignettes from Trains in Motion.* In addition, she is a World Fantasy Award–winning illustrator, has previously been a translator and a lawyer, and holds both an MPhil and PhD in creative writing (Australian Gothic literature and creative observation, respectively).